D0724273

MORGANTOWN
373 SPRUCE STREET
MORGANTOWN

01:37PM

MPKA, SARAH PAT

e bachelors c

you
01510001024441
DATE: 07-08-21

TITLE: Stay with me

$ 5.00

MORGANTOWN PUBLIC LIBRARY
373 SPRUCE STREET
MORGANTOWN, WV 26505

13 2 01 20

By Monica Murphy

The Billionaire Bachelors Club Series
Crave

New Adult
Second Chance Boyfriend
One Week Girlfriend

PUBLIC LIBRARY

WV 26505

Crave

Crave

A BILLIONAIRE BACHELORS
CLUB NOVEL

MONICA MURPHY

MORGANTOWN PUBLIC LIBRARY
373 SPRUCE STREET
MORGANTOWN, WV 26505

AVONIMPULSE
An Imprint of HarperCollinsPublishers

This is a work of fiction. Names, characters, places, and incidents are products of the author's imagination or are used fictitiously and are not to be construed as real. Any resemblance to actual events, locales, organizations, or persons, living or dead, is entirely coincidental.

Excerpt from *Torn* copyright © 2013 by Karen Erickson.

Excerpt from *Less Than a Gentleman* copyright © 2013 by Kerrelyn Sparks.

Excerpt from *When I Find You* copyright © 2013 by Dixie Brown.

Excerpt from *Playing the Field* copyright © 2013 by Candice Wakoff.

Excerpt from *How to Marry a Highlander* copyright © 2013 by Katharine Brophy Dubois.

CRAVE. Copyright © 2013 by Karen Erickson. All rights reserved under International and Pan-American Copyright Conventions. By payment of the required fees, you have been granted the non-exclusive, nontransferable right to access and read the text of this e-book on screen. No part of this text may be reproduced, transmitted, decompiled, reverse-engineered, or stored in or introduced into any information storage and retrieval system, in any form or by any means, whether electronic or mechanical, now known or hereinafter invented, without the express written permission of HarperCollins e-books.

EPub Edition AUGUST 2013 ISBN: 9780062289346

Print Edition ISBN: 9780062289353

JV 10 9 8 7 6 5 4 3 2 1

Chapter One

Archer

THERE ARE FEW things I can resist in life. This is probably why I got into so much trouble during my younger years. Control is everything—and that is the one thing I've learned from my bastard of a father. You gain nothing by letting yourself go, by revealing your emotions, by becoming vulnerable.

If you're unable to resist the things that draw you in, it's a surefire way to ask for unwanted chaos. I've had enough of that in my personal life growing up. Hell, in my professional life too, though I've finally turned that corner these last few years.

But the few things I can't resist? A challenge. A bet.

"He's an absolute sucker to get married," Gage says, his disgust-filled voice pulling me from my thoughts. Gage Emerson is my best friend. Matt DeLuca is too. I've known them both since high school. We're standing together at our college buddy Jeff Lewiston's wedding reception, lurking in a dark corner of the crowded ballroom and muttering over the so-called sanctity of marriage.

Marriage represents a noose around my neck that tightens with every miserable day. My parents are a shining example of the worst marriage in the history of marriages. They hate each other. They cheat on each other. They fight. Yet they're still together.

Makes no damn sense.

"He seems happy," Matt, the more optimistic of us three, starts, and both Gage and I shoot him a look that shuts him up.

"His wife is attractive, I'll give her that," Gage concedes, sipping from his glass of champagne. "But the moment they come back from the Tahitian honeymoon, she'll turn into the biggest bitch on the planet, I guarantee it."

"You don't even know her," Matt mutters, shaking his head.

"Don't have to. They all do it. Sexy and beautiful and sweet when you first meet them, you don't know what to think. The sex is amazing and you're having it constantly. They'll drop to their knees whenever you ask and give you a grade-A blowjob. Next thing you know, you're buying them a ring." Gage pauses, takes another swig of his champagne, draining the glass.

We've talked about this before. We've watched our friends go down one by one like fallen soldiers to marriage, especially this last year.

"You get that ring on their finger, go through this

whole marriage ceremony bullshit and then you're left with nothing but a nagging wife and a limp dick in the aftermath. Always giving you shit because you're never home and you work too much." I grimace because holy hell, that sounds like my worst nightmare.

"They sure as hell never complain when they're spending your money, though." Gage gestures with his empty glass.

"Hear, motherfucking-hear," I say, returning the gesture with my glass before I finish it off.

"You guys are such cynics. Both of you act like you've done this sort of thing before." Matt crosses his arms in front of his chest. "When was the last time either of you had a girlfriend." He doesn't phrase it as a question because he already knows the answer.

"Never," I sneer. Serious girlfriends aren't a consideration. None of them interested me enough to want to keep them around.

With the exception of one woman and I absolutely cannot touch her. She's too young, too sweet, too good, too everything I'm not. She's so fucking tempting and so completely off limits, I'd be a damn fool to attempt anything with her.

But I want to. Desperately.

"All this talk about how a woman is nothing but shackles and chains like some sort of lifetime prison sentence. I can't wait to see you both fall and fall fucking hard." Matt laughed.

Gage and I both glare. "I have no plans of falling any time soon," Gage mutters.

"More like never in this lifetime," I add.

"Please." Matt snorts. "You'll both eventually realize you don't want to do this thing called 'life' without a woman by your side. Then you'll be scrambling at some ungodly age, like forty-five, the eternal bachelors looking for some hot piece to be your bride. None of those young babes in their twenties will look at you unless you flash some cash their way."

"Now who's the cynic," I retort, earning a glare from Matt.

"I speak the truth," he says with a shrug. "And you know it."

"You bag on us for being single, yet you're single too," Gage points out. "Why haven't you settled down yet?"

Gage's question earns another shrug from Matt. "Haven't found the right woman yet."

His answer is so simple and sounds so damn logical I want to smack him.

"There is no right woman," I say, wanting to burst Matt's happily-ever-after bubble. "You'll eventually settle. Trust me."

"And you won't," Gage says, though I know he's not disagreeing with me. "I know I don't plan on settling. I don't plan on tying myself down whatsoever."

"Neither do I," I agree. "Settling is for pussies."

"Absolutely," Gage says grimly.

Matt focuses his attention solely on me. "I'll bet big money you'll be the first to go down."

"Go down how? On a woman?" This earns a laugh from Gage. "Go down in flames? What the hell are you talking about?"

"You'll be the first to fall in love with a woman and beg her to marry you," Matt says.

My mouth goes dry. It feels like an invisible noose just tightened around my neck, making it hard to breathe. "Yeah, right," I finally manage to choke out.

"You two are so damn resistant to being a relationship, I figure you'll both be slapped upside the head and fall hard. And it's going to happen sooner rather than later," Matt says, his voice full of confidence.

That smug tone irritates the hell out of me.

"There is no way I'll fall in love anytime soon," I say.

"Me either," Gage agrees.

"If you guys want to believe that, then cool. Live in your world of denial, I don't care." Our friend is trying to piss us off. And it's working.

"You wanna make that bet you just mentioned? Because I'm in. I'll prove it to you. I don't need a woman or a relationship." I cross my arms in front of my chest. Matt's done this before. He enjoys getting a rise out of the both of us. Drives me crazy.

So let's see if he goes for it. Always running that mouth of his. Time to put up or shut up.

Gage snorts. "Don't just bet him. Let's all three get in on this one."

"How much we talking?" Matt scrubs his hand along his jaw. The guy is loaded. We're all loaded; we come from wealthy families and we lived in the same neighborhood during high school. When we all turned twenty-one within a few months of each other, we started going to Vegas and dropping big money like a regular person plays the quarter slots. Once we graduated college and got real lives, we had to stop that shit. I still miss it. Sort of.

"A million bucks to the last single man standing," Gage throws out, a triumphant gleam in his eye. He acts like he's already won the prize.

"A million dollars?" Matt's eyes practically bug out of his head. Asshole acts like he's not good for it despite having to recently bow out of a lucrative pro baseball contract due to a career-ending injury—and he didn't lose a dollar of that contract either. The guy has buckets full of money. He recently invested some of it in a winery not far from where I live just so he could claim a loss for his taxes.

He's definitely not hurting financially. Neither is Gage. He's one of the top real estate investors in all the Bay Area, right behind his father. They both have the magic touch, finding properties and businesses for a song and turning them around for a tremendous profit.

The hotel industry claims I have the magic touch as well, despite my father's irritation at that particular assertion. I can't help that I saw a need and filled it with the loser hotel he gave me. He firmly believed I'd fail.

I proved him wrong. Hell, I'm getting ready to expand. And he hates that.

It's almost as if my own father would relish seeing me fail.

"What, you scared?" I say this because I know there is no way in hell I will lose this bet. No woman can sink her claws into me so deep I can't escape.

No way, no how.

Gage laughs and shakes his head. "Don't be such a pussy, DeLuca. A million bucks is chump change in your bank account."

"Not really," Matt mutters. "Not that I'm worried. I'll win."

Ha. Matt making that confident of a statement pushes me to prove him wrong. "You really think so?"

"I know so." Matt smiles. "I'd even bet an extra fifty grand the next woman you talk to, you'll end up marrying."

"Sucker bet, bro. Take him up on it," Gage chimes in, nudging my shoulder hard. "Give us a break, Matt. I can't think of one woman in this entire room Archer would want to talk to, let alone *marry*."

I remain quiet. There is one woman I wouldn't mind talking to. Spend time with. Not in the serious sense or the potential marriage sense, because hell no, that's not in my future. I'd make some poor woman a terrible husband and I know it. Which is why I leave her alone.

She wants that sort of thing. A husband and kids and a white picket fence around the pretty little house she decorated. I know she does. She's a dreamer, a romantic, a woman who deserves to be treated like a queen. I'd only end up hurting her and I couldn't live with myself if I did. Gage wouldn't let me live either.

He knows her well, considering I'm referring to his baby sister.

Once upon a time, when she was younger, I thought of her like a baby sister too. But then she blossomed into this hot teenager that had me thinking all the wrong thoughts every time I got near her. Seventeen-year-old Ivy made me feel like a pervert. Didn't help that every time I tried to avoid her, she wanted to talk to me. As if she knew she drove me crazy and was determined to get under my skin with her sweet, thoughtful ways, how she laughed at my jokes and looked at me as if she could see right through me.

And when she grew into this beautiful, sexy, confident woman, I knew without a doubt I had to avoid her at all costs. I wanted to be with her in the worst damn way. She's the first woman I ever truly cared for. I don't want to hurt her, because I would. I hurt all the women in my life. Ask my mother. Ask any female who thought she had a fleeting chance at being with me.

"Maybe you could go babysit Ivy for a little while," Gage suggests.

I turn to him, incredulous. Can he reach inside my brain and read my thoughts? Fucking scary how he just did that.

"What do you mean?" I ask warily.

"You want to win an easy fifty grand? Go be with Ivy. Like she'd marry your sorry ass." Gage laughs, though I don't. Why am I a sorry ass? Yeah, I know I'm not worthy of Ivy, but damn, his words still hurt.

When I don't say anything, Gage continues.

"She broke it off with the guy she'd been seeing a few nights ago. Not that he was worthy of her, but she's been down in the dumps ever since," Gage explains. "You could go hang out with her for the rest of the night, use her to fight off any other female who might approach. Ivy's always liked you, though I don't know why since you're such a jackass." He pauses, his eyes narrowed. "I realize you enjoy chasing everything in a skirt, but I know you won't take advantage of my sister. Right?"

The pointed look he gives me rings loud and clear. I want to promise him I won't take advantage of her. But he's talking about Ivy . . . and I always want what I can't have.

Especially her.

"She doesn't count anyway," Matt says with a chuckle. "After all, it's just Ivy."

"Right. Just Ivy." I nod as I look around, hoping to spot her. She's here. I saw her earlier, though she avoided me. Most of the time, I choose to aggravate the shit out of her rather than let on how I really feel. "You mean she doesn't count toward that crazy-ass bet you just made me?'

"Yeah, she totally doesn't count. Besides, Gage would kill you," Matt says matter-of-factly. "There are approximately twenty-five women spying on us at this very moment, all of them sorority sisters or whatever of the bride. They're dying for you to even look their way, Archer. First one that talks to you, I guarantee you'll marry."

"Bullshit," I mumble. My friend has lost his damn mind.

"Whatever." Matt laughs as does Gage, but I ignore them.

Glancing across the room, I see her. Ivy. Sitting at a table alone, watching couples sway together on the dance floor to some sappy love song. Her long, brown hair is wavy when she usually wears it straight, and I'm tempted to run my hands through it, see if it feels as silky soft as it looks. Her dress is a rich, dark blue and strapless, revealing plenty of smooth, creamy flesh that my fingers literally itch to touch.

The wistful longing on her face is obvious and I'm compelled to go to her. Ask her to dance. Pull her in close, feel her curves mold against me as I breathe in her sweet scent.

Damn.

Yeah. She'd probably tell me to go to hell before she'd dance with me.

"I don't want to touch her," I say, which is a lie because I would fucking love to touch her. "You can trust me."

More lies. Gage should kick me in the nuts just for thinking about his sister. Let alone actually doing something to her. With her. Over her, under her, any way I can get her. She's the only one who could tempt me to break the crazy bet I just made. Who could make me want to go against everything I've ever believed in since I was a kid.

But I won't. I refuse to give in. She's not for me.

No matter how badly I want her to be.

Ivy

THERE'S NOTHING WORSE than going to a wedding alone, especially when I'd had a date approximately forty-eight hours ago. Before I realized the guy I was seeing was also still seeing the woman he claimed he'd broke up with well over six months ago.

How did I find out this amazingly bad news? The supposed ex called my cell and chewed me out while I was looking over wallpaper samples with a client. Talk about humiliating. Talk about my life turning into a Jerry Springer episode. She made me feel like a cheating whore-bag out to steal her man, the very last thing I am. I am not a man-stealer. I know some women are attracted to men in relationships but not me. Taken men are too much trouble, thank you very much.

I hung up on the still-ranting, supposed ex-girlfriend and promptly called Marc, letting him know I couldn't see him any longer. He'd hardly protested—no surprise. What a jerk.

So now I sit here alone. At the single and dateless table, because when I called the bride and told her I wasn't bringing my date after all, Cecily flipped out. Claimed I would mess up her carefully orchestrated seating arrangement and *oh my God, couldn't you just bring your date anyway and deal?*

I think my saying an emphatic *no* resulted in me ending up at the desperate and single section as punishment.

Sighing, I prop my elbow on the edge of the table and rest my chin on my fist, watching all the couples dancing, the bride and groom in the center of the floor, grinning up at each other like fools. They look happy. Everyone looks happy.

I'm jealous of all the happiness surrounding me. Weddings remind me I'm alone. For once, I wish I could find someone. I've had a string of bad luck with men my entire dating life. I pick wrong, my mom has told me more than once. She describes me as a fixer. I take the broken guys and try to put them back together again. "Humpty Dumpty syndrome" is what she calls it.

Gee, thanks, Mom.

My brother says I'm too young to want to settle down, but I'm nothing like him. He just wants to screw around and stay single forever. Gage doesn't know what I want. Do I though? I'm not sure. I thought I did. I thought Marc had potential.

Turns out he went splat all over the ground. Definitely couldn't put him back together again.

Maybe I shouldn't take everything so damn seriously. Maybe I should let loose and do something completely and totally crazy. Like find some random guy and make out with him in a dark corner. I miss having a man cup my face and kiss me slowly. Thoroughly. Unfortunately, Marc wasn't that great of a kisser. Too much thrusting tongue, though I firmly believed I could help him correct that annoying habit.

He didn't give me a chance, which is fine, because really, chemistry is everything. If I don't feel a spark with a kiss, then the guy is clearly not right for me.

If I'm going to consider a relationship with a guy, that's what I want. What I need. A spark. Chemistry. A few stolen kisses, wandering hands, whispered words in a quiet corner where someone might catch us. He'd press me up against a wall, cradle my face in his hands, and kiss me like he means it . . .

I frown. I'm sitting alone contemplating a wild wedding reception hookup with a faceless guy. Since when did I become so desperate?

"I'd say, for letting you go so easily."

Did he really just say that? What did he mean? "Is there something you wanted to talk about?" I'm eager to get rid of him. For whatever reason, with only a few words he's confusing me tonight and I don't like it. I'm confused enough, what with my secret wishes for random hookups with hot guys.

Hot like Archer . . .

"Yeah, there is." The smile returns, gentler now, not full of the usual bravado. "Want to dance?"

"With you?" I'm incredulous. And I want to laugh when I see he's obviously offended by my question.

"Yeah, with me. Come on." He holds out his hand. "Be my shield before some crazy woman tries to drag me out onto the dance floor. They're circling, chicken. They're about to jump me if I don't watch it."

He's right. I can see a few women starting to approach us. Suddenly overcome with the need to let them know that he's not available, I let him take my hand, his long fingers clasping around mine as he pulls me to my feet. He blatantly checks me out, his gaze running down the length of my body, lingering on my chest, and I simultaneously want to punch him and ask if he likes what he sees.

Yeah, definitely confusing.

A woman appears before us, her smile so wide I wonder if it hurts her face. "Hey, you're Archer Bancroft, right? From Bancroft Hotels? The Hush Resort and Spa?" she asks, her voice falsely bright.

"I am." He pulls me closer, releasing my hand so he

can wrap his arm around my shoulders in a proprietary way, like he's claiming me. His thumb rubs circles against my skin, making my breaths come a little faster, and I drop my gaze to the floor, trying to gather my composure. "Have we met before?"

"Once. Long ago, but I'm sure you don't remember me." I glance up and watch as her smile grows. How is that even possible? "I've always wanted to go there. To Hush."

Hush Resort and Spa. The hotel Archer's father gave him as some sort of punishment after he barely graduated college. He turned it into one of the most exclusive and successful couples-only resorts in all the country, if not the world. He became white-hot in an instant, in demand. Gorgeous and sexy, intelligent and ruthless, women wanted to do him, men wanted to be him. And the arrogant jackass knew it.

"I suggest you make a reservation." His voice is full of irritation. He's trying to steer us around her but she's not budging.

"I can't. I'm not part of a couple." She literally bats her eyelashes. "Maybe you could help with that?"

"I'm sure we could find one of your friends to hook her up with, don't you think, baby?" I smile up at Archer, sending him a meaningful look so he gets what I'm trying to do. He blinks down at me, no doubt startled by being called baby, which is fun. He's sort of hot when he's confused, and it's hard to frazzle Archer. So I decide to do it some more.

Leaning up, I nuzzle his neck, inhaling his unique

spicy scent. God, he smells amazing. Why have I never noticed this before? Not that we're ever standing this close together, but I'm tempted to rub against him like a cat.

I wonder if she's bought we're a couple yet. If I have to keep this up I might do something crazy. Like . . . bite him. "I'm sure that could be arranged," he says, his voice rough as his arm tightens around my shoulders.

I slip my arm around his back. He's as solid as a rock. Makes me wonder what he looks like beneath all the finery. I haven't seen him shirtless since I was in high school, and he's filled out since then considerably. "If you'll excuse us," I tell Miss Persistent with a sickeningly sweet smile before I turn it on Archer. "Let's go dance, baby."

He leads me out onto the dance floor wordlessly, pulling me into his arms just as another slow song starts. His hand rests on the small of my back as we begin to move to the music and my entire body tingles at his nearness. Which is odd because 1. I have no desire to be with Archer like that and 2. I've been immune to his charm for years.

Weird.

"You're good, with the 'baby' bit and rubbing your nose against my neck," he murmurs close to my ear. His hot breath makes me shiver and I wonder if he felt it. He had to.

And I don't really care. I'm hyperaware of him, of his size and his warmth and the sheer strength of him. His big hand shifts lower on my back, his fingertips grazing my backside, and I inhale sharply. I bet he knows just how to use those hands, too.

Oh my God, this is Archer you're drooling over. Stop it!

"Think she bought our act?" I ask breathlessly.

"Not sure." He hesitates for the slightest moment, causing me to look up at him. I'm struck dumb by his smoldering gaze, the way he's staring at me like he wants to gobble me up. I wonder if I'm returning the same look, because I have the sudden urge to kiss him. For hours, if possible. "But I know I did."

Chapter Two

Archer

WELL, THAT WAS totally unexpected.

I'm still reeling, though I'm trying my damnedest to act like she doesn't affect me whatsoever. All that "It's just Ivy" talk flew right out the window when I saw the glint of determination in her gaze as she realized she could help me get rid of the clingy woman. How she draped herself all over me and called me baby. Flashing me a sexy, secretive smile as if she knew exactly what I looked like naked and liked it.

Then she went and nuzzled my neck with her nose, making me so hard I'm still aching with the memory just before she moved away.

Talk about torture. No wonder I avoid her. Within a few minutes of being near her, I'm sporting wood and plotting how I can get her out of here so I can strip her naked and have my way with her. All night long.

"You're teasing me," she chastises, her pretty hazel eyes watching me carefully as we dance. There aren't many couples on the floor but the bride and groom are nearby, the lights are dimmed low, and the atmosphere is scarily romantic. "You so didn't buy into that act. Come on."

Fuck, she's the tease. I'm not sure she gets just how much she affects me. I know she doesn't. I wonder if she ever thinks of me. Her brother's best friend, the jerk wad who does nothing but give her a bunch of crap. Knowing her since I was sixteen seems to translate me into my idiot teenage self every time I'm around her. It's like I can't help it.

I'm a grown-ass man worth billions who runs one of the most successful, exclusive resorts in the country and this is what Ivy Emerson reduces me to.

"I pretty much did buy into it," I offer with a shrug. Going for nonchalant. "I'm surprised you didn't take it to the next level. Grab my dick and claim it as yours."

A dark brow rose, her lips quirked to the side. Damn, she's hot, even when she's irritated. Especially when she's irritated. "You are so crude."

If only she knew the extent of my so-called crudeness. I want her.

Having her in my arms is not helping my plight, but she's soft and she smells so damn good I can't resist her. Her dark hair shines beneath the golden lights and the top of her strapless dress appears fairly easy to tug down if I wanted to do such a thing.

Not that I do. Not really.

Liar.

It's not just her beauty that does me in though. There's so much more to Ivy. How she listens to me, how proud she seems to be when I tell her what I'm doing in my career. It's like she really cares.

"You've always appreciated my blunt honesty," I assure her, pulling her in just the slightest bit closer as I twirl her around the dance floor. Her breasts brush against my chest, her hand slides over my shoulder, and her touch burns me. Through my suit jacket and shirt, like she's touching bare flesh, branding me.

And I want to be branded by her. Despite my reluctance of ever becoming involved with a woman, Ivy's the only one who I both want to be with and want to run away from.

Yeah. I make no damn sense.

"Really? According to whom? When was the last time we had a scintillating conversation, hmm?" She smiles. It's faint but there, and the sight of it encourages me.

Plus, she just made the word *scintillating* sound hot. The woman is either some sort of sex goddess or I've turned into a complete pervert. "Maybe we need to renew our friendship. Get to know each other again," I suggest, trying my best to sound nonchalant.

"Like you care about getting to know me again." She rolls her eyes. "We've known each other for years. It's not like you've ever shown any sort of interest in me before."

"I've always been interested, you just never noticed." I pause, taking in the way her eyes widen the slightest bit. I bet my revelation surprises her. "Every time I see you, Ivy, I remember what you looked like when you were twelve, the first time I met you. All gangly and skinny with braces." Look at her now. She's filled out in all the right places and she's the sexiest woman at this stupid reception.

"Great. So you see me as an eternal twelve-year-old," she mutters, curling her lip.

Shit. I've somehow stepped in it with a few choice words. Could I be more of an idiot?

"I definitely don't see you as a twelve-year-old," I murmur, tightening my hold on her hand. "You have to realize that, right?"

She meets my gaze, her eyes full of wariness, her pouty lips curved in the tiniest frown. "What do you see me as, Archer? Gage's pain-in-the-ass little sister? The girl you made fun of her freshman year when you were a mighty senior? Remember how you did that?"

Well hell, is she going to list all of my faults or what? I'm not proud of the way I acted when I was younger. I'd been a self-centered bastard. Some say I still am. "I was a jackass back then," I mutter.

"From what I've observed, you're still holding on to some of those jackass tendencies." Her hazel eyes flash as she lifts her chin in subtle defiance.

"What's that supposed to mean?" Damn, maybe I avoid her because we tend to argue every time we're around each other. Yet I want her. I've wanted her for what feels like forever. But she acts like she despises me. Like my very presence fills her with disgust. No other woman has reacted to me like this—ever. I don't get it.

I don't get her. And I definitely don't get my attraction to her.

Glutton for punishment maybe?

Yeah. I shove that nagging little voice straight to the back of my brain.

"Forget it." Her gaze cuts away from mine.

"Tell me what you're talking about, Ivy."

"Nothing." She meets my gaze once more. "Drop it, okay?"

I let her drop it and we dance quietly, the sharks still circling. I can spot at least three women who are contemplating me standing on the edge of the dance floor. Ready to jump on me the moment the song is over.

I gotta get out of here.

"Let's go outside," I tell Ivy, my gaze trained on one woman in particular who's vaguely familiar. I swear the groom tried to set me up with her once. We went out to some dinner when Jeff and Cecily were first dating.

"Are you serious? No way will I go outside with you. You'll probably try to maul me."

That sounds like a fantastic idea but I know she won't go for it. "Maybe you need a good mauling to get that stick out of your ass."

"What did you just say?" She stops dancing so abruptly she nearly trips over my feet, what with those fuck-me high heels she's wearing.

Tightening my arm around her waist, I save her from sprawling. "I speak the truth and you know it. You need to loosen up, chicken. No wonder the last guy didn't stick, what with how uptight you are." Her eyes widen and her jaw drops open. She looks ready to tear into me and I immediately regret what I said. "Ivy, I'm sorry," I start, but she cuts me off.

"Fuck you," she whispers harshly, shoving at me so I have no choice but to let go of her and watch as she escapes the dance floor.

A woman swoops in within seconds, the same one Jeff tried to hook me up with long ago. I remember she had stalkerish qualities, what with the way she Googled me prior to going out to dinner. I know it's the norm nowadays but her admission turned me off. "Archer. It's so good to see you again. Want to dance?"

I glance toward the open doors that lead onto the giant terrace. Ivy's headed straight toward them, her hips swaying, her legs looking incredibly long. She's gorgeous and sexy as fuck and I said she needed to get the stick out of her ass.

What the hell is wrong with me?

"Archer?"

I turn my attention to the woman who's looking at me expectantly. I don't even remember her name. Ivy's right. I still have plenty of assholeish tendencies and I just unleashed them all over her. "Sorry, I'm going to have to pass. I need to go apologize to a woman."

Ivy

THE MOMENT I'M outside, I take a deep, gulping breath, the cold air filling my lungs, kissing my skin, and making me shiver. I'm angry, but thankfully the air cools my heated emotions and I lean against the railing that overlooks the golf course, happy no one else is around. Considering I'm in the farthest corner of the terrace from the open doors of the ballroom, that's no surprise.

I still can't believe what Archer said to me. He is the biggest jerk on the planet, I swear to God. He actually said I have a stick up my ass. I mean, what the hell? Could he hurl any more insults at me? Oh wait, I'm sure he can.

No wonder I always avoid him. This is what usually happens between Archer and me whenever we spend any time together. I try to be nice. He's his usual jerky self. I get defensive. He insults me. We argue. We then avoid each other until for whatever reason we're forced to see each other again.

We're like a broken record. No matter what, we can't get along. He is the most frustrating person I've ever met. He drives me crazy. And that I'm in his territory tonight, in Napa Valley where his resort is located—not too far, as a matter of fact—also makes me uneasy. Why, I'm not sure.

I wish I were back home in San Francisco, in my comfort zone. At my little apartment, where I'd watch a movie while contemplating going to bed early on another exciting Saturday night.

Frowning, I sigh heavily and hang my head. I've turned into this pitiful, dateless creature all in a matter of hours. What confuses me more? That despite our arguing and the constant animosity that brews between Archer and me, I felt something else between us earlier? Something I would never dare contemplate before?

Sexual attraction.

Tilting my head back, I drink in the night sky. Away from the city lights, I can actually see the stars and there are a bazillion of them stretched across the night's velvety blackness. They twinkle at me, full of mystery and hope and opportunity.

My life is good. I shouldn't let guys hang it up and make me miserable. Marc is a jerk who happened to be a bad kisser. Archer is an asshole who could probably kiss the pants off of me, but I won't go there.

Damn it, I should be happy. I'm working my dream job as an interior designer under one of the best designers in all of San Francisco. I have my own apartment—no more living with my parents, and thankfully no more college roommates. I have great friends and a supportive family. I shouldn't let this sort of thing bother me.

But what Archer said . . . it bothers me. I don't have a stick up my ass, do I? I'm not uptight. I swear I'm not uptight.

Maybe I can be a little controlling, but never stick-in-the-ass uptight . . .

Whipping out my phone, I send my friend Wendy a quick text and wait anxiously for her reply.

She responds in seconds, which impresses me since I know she's out on a date tonight.

No, you're NOT uptight. Who told you that? Let me gues . . . Marc. What an asshole.

Laughing, I shake my head. I appreciate her immediate defense of me. That's what friends are for, right?

Not Marc, I respond. *Someone else. Someone I've known since high school.*

Since I met Wendy in college, I don't think I've mentioned Archer to her, have I? God, I don't know. We talk about all sorts of stuff. She's my closest friend.

So of course I've mentioned Archer to her.

One of your brother's friends? She texts back.

Yeah.

Which one? Let me guess . . . Archer Bancroft. He's hot. But he also must be a complete asshole for calling you uptight.

Laughing, I type her a quick reply. "Isn't that the truth," I mutter.

"Isn't what the truth?"

Gasping, I whirl around to see Archer standing there, his hands shoved in his pockets and looking absolutely miserable.

Good.

Oh, and also absolutely gorgeous, which sucks. Why, oh why, did this man have to be so handsome?

"That you're an asshole?" I smile as serenely as possible, ignoring the buzz of my phone indicating I have another text. I shove it in the pocket of my dress, thankful it came with one. A girl and her phone can never part.

"Listen, I came out here to tell you I'm sorry." He runs a hand through his hair, messing it up completely. Which of course makes him even sexier, and that's so unfair it's ridiculous. "It's just . . . every time we're together, we somehow end up arguing."

"I can't help it if you're rude," I say with a sniff. I sound like a complete snot but I don't care.

"You push all my buttons," he admits, his voice quiet and edged with a mysterious darkness that sends a thrill shooting down my spine. He keeps his eyes trained on me as he slowly draws closer.

"Right back at you." Why do I sound so breathless? It doesn't help that he's stopped directly in front of me, his big, broad body obliterating everything else until he's all I can see.

"I'm hoping you'll find it in your heart to forgive me." He reaches out his hand toward me and I stare at it, not sure what he wants me to do. "Please?"

Did Archer Bancroft just say *please*? I'm sure this is a rare moment in history. "Why do you care about having my forgiveness?" I keep my gaze trained on his hand for fear he'll see the confusion and emotion in my eyes.

Shit. What is wrong with me?

"Fuck, Ivy, why do you always have to be so difficult?" His hand drops.

I chance looking up at him, see the irritation and frustration written all over his face and I'm so overcome with the need to comfort him I take a step forward, ready to grab hold of his hand and . . .

And what?

"Archer?" A woman's voice calls from nearby, causing the both of us to look at each other. The slightly panicked look on his face indicates he knows exactly who this woman is.

"Who's looking for you?" I ask.

"No one."

I raise an eyebrow. "Clearly someone is, since I can hear her call your name."

"She's not important. I went on one dinner date with her, Jeff, and Cecily a long time ago. She had us married and planning for babies by the end of it," he says irritably, glancing over his shoulder.

"What's her name?"

He turns to me. "What?"

"Her name? The no one who's looking for you?"

"I, uh . . . don't remember." He runs a hand through that sexy hair again, strands falling over his forehead, and I'm filled with the sudden urge to push his hair out of his eyes. Comb my fingers through it.

Stop!

I need to remember he's a complete jackass. I should run. Right now. In fact, I'm fully preparing to let him know exactly how much of an ass I think he is when the woman's voice sounds again, closer this time as she continues to call Archer's name like some worried owner looking for her pet dog.

"We should—*oh*."

He practically shoves me against the railing, the rough concrete scratching my back through the thin fabric of my dress and he immediately slips his arm around my waist, protecting me. Holding me. His chest is against mine, my breasts pressed flush to him, and I release a skittering breath, my mind hung up on having him too close.

"What are you doing?" I whisper, incredulous.

"Shh." He rests his hand over my mouth, silencing me.

His palm is big and warm, his fingers long, and I swear his skin tastes the slightest bit salty, not that I'm licking him or anything.

Oh God, I think ... no, I *know* I want to lick him. Desperately. Slip one of those long fingers in between my lips and suck. And that is just so, so wrong ...

"Maybe she won't find us," he whispers, dipping his head so his gaze meets mine. "Stay still."

I slowly nod, his hand still over my mouth, his eyes locked with mine. His touch gentles as he takes another step closer and I want to melt at his nearness.

"Archer, are you back here?"

I flick my eyes to the left and see the woman. She's standing about fifty feet away, her head whipping this way and that, almost frantically searching, and I press farther against the ledge at the same time Archer steps into me. His arm is still around my waist, protecting me from the rough concrete, and he's standing so close I can hardly breathe.

There's a giant pine tree giving us cover, throwing shadows over the corner we're standing in, and I don't think the woman can really see us. She's oblivious to the fact we're not that far from her.

Which I'm thankful for. I shouldn't be. I should be kicking Archer in the shins and letting the woman know he's right here and then throwing him to the she-wolf. Let him deal with the poor soul he rejected God knows how long ago who still harbors a thing for him.

He's a complete womanizer. I'd be wise to stay away from him.

My head tells me this. But my body is singing a completely different tune.

Our gazes lock, his thumb sweeps back and forth across my cheek so slowly I want to die. It feels so good. This . . . is not right. His nearness confuses me. The way he looks at me, touches me, it makes me want him.

Desperately.

My earlier thoughts come rushing back, when I was being all "woe-is-me" wishing for a random stranger to make out with in a dark corner. Being with Archer like this is the next best thing. He's looking at me like he's thinking the same thing I am. Which is scary.

Exhilarating. Exciting.

As I stare up at him, I see how absolutely perfect his lips are. How come I never noticed this before? And when his tongue darts out to lick them, why are my knees suddenly shaking?

Oh, this is bad. So, so bad.

The woman finally gives up and leaves and I slump against the railing, ready for him to move away from me. Ready for him to grab me by the hips and lift me up onto the concrete ledge so I can wrap my legs around him and beg him to do me.

Wait, what? I so can't do that. Clearly, I've had too much to drink, if two glasses of champagne could be considered excessive drinking. Which it must be, because I am making absolutely no sense.

"Ivy . . ." His hand slips from my mouth to cup my cheek, his thumb drifting across the corner of my lips. "I'm sorry."

His touch distracts me as I try to frown. He's doing everything I longed for not even an hour ago. Touching my face, nestled against me in a dark corner where anyone could find us. "What are you apologizing for?"

He cradles my face with his big, warm hands and dips his head, his gaze locked on my mouth for a long, breathless moment before he lifts his lids, his dark eyes meeting mine. "This," he whispers just before he kisses me.

Chapter Three

Archer

I TAKE IT slow for fear Ivy will push me away, and at this very moment that's the last thing I want to happen. Her lips part easily when I persist and within moments she's completely open to me, her tongue sliding against mine. She winds her arms around my neck, her fingers buried in my hair, and I groan at her touch.

Slow goes straight out the window when I smooth my hand down her side, over her hip, curling my fingers into the fabric of her dress. I hitch it up the slightest bit, my mouth never straying from hers, and I feel her tremble beneath my palm as I slip my hand beneath her skirt.

She tastes amazing, feels even better, and when I touch the bare flesh of her thigh I feel her shudder, a soft gust of breath brushing against my lips as she shakily exhales.

Her eyes open and meet mine as I smooth my other hand over her hair, fingers tangling in the loose waves.

"You're beautiful," I whisper, because she is. So damn beautiful, I ache with wanting her.

She presses her swollen lips together, her eyes closing as I continue to stroke my fingers through her hair. My other hand is completely still, resting on the outside of her thigh beneath her skirt, and I don't move for fear she'll tell me to let her go.

I don't know if I can.

"Archer," she whispers, and I kiss her to cut off whatever else she wanted to say. If it was a denial, an argument, a declaration, I don't care. I don't want to hear it.

I just want to feel Ivy in my arms, her mouth meshed with mine, our tongues dancing, her entire body trembling as she melts into me. I've waited for this moment for what feels like forever.

Finally, I'm holding her. Finally, she's responding to me like she wants me rather than wanting to kick my ass. While the opportunity presents itself, I'm going to jump all over it. And if that means I get to jump all over Ivy, then I'm going for it.

I let my hand on her thigh inch upward, slowly. Closer to her hip until my fingers skim the lacy scrap of her panties and my dick twitches behind my zipper. The fabric is thin and doesn't amount to much and I wish I could push her against the ledge, yank her skirt up to her waist, and drink her in.

But we only have a few minutes. I'm desperate to

touch her. To make her gasp with wanting me, so I have to be quick.

My mouth never straying from hers, I slip my fingers beneath the thin strip that stretches across her hip and touch bare, soft flesh. Her chest heaves against mine, her breasts pushing into my chest and adrenaline rushes through me at the way she reacts to my touch.

That reaction emboldens me and I trail my fingers forward, across her hipbone, the soft flesh of her stomach. I can feel the tremors beneath the surface of her skin as I skim my fingers down farther . . . farther . . . until the heat of her engulfs me and I slowly slip my hand between her legs.

"Archer," she chokes out against my lips when I touch her, test her. She's drenched, so wet my fingers glide easily over her folds.

"Damn, you're wet." She grips my shoulders as if she needs to. Like I'm some sort of lifeline and she's afraid to let go. "Tell me what you want," I whisper close to her ear, my fingers between her legs, searching her hot, wet depths. She moves with me, her hips thrusting against my hand and I close my eyes, fighting for control. Scared out of my mind I'm going to come in my pants and make a fool of myself.

She says nothing in reply, just a little whimper when I still my hand, my thumb resting on her clit. "Tell me, Ivy."

"Touch me." She tightens her arms around my neck, her hands clenching my hair. "Don't stop. Please."

Satisfaction rolls through me as I try my damnedest to make her come and quick. We're on the terrace of my friend's wedding reception for Christ's sake. Her brother—my best friend—is inside. Gage could come out at any time in search of us.

If he caught me with my hand in his sister's panties and her body draped all over me, I'd be a dead man.

Increasing my tempo, I stroke her clit, watch her face as she reaches for her orgasm. She's so responsive, already close to coming, I can tell, what with the way her entire body tenses, her hands squeezing my shoulders, her hips moving against my touch. I tilt my head back to watch her, filled with the all-consuming need to see her as she comes all over my hand. Knowing that I'm the one who did that to her. Made her feel like that. Made her want like that.

Me.

A ragged little cry escapes her and she stills, her eyes going wide as they lock with mine. Then she's coming apart, sagging against me as the orgasm takes over her completely. My name falls from her lips and triumph surges through me. I fucking love it. At least she knows I'm the one who did this to her, who made her feel this way.

Shudders still wrack her body as I lock my mouth with hers, my tongue tangling languidly with hers. Her breaths slow, her grip on my shoulders gradually loosens, and I know she's coming down off her high.

I don't want her to lose it. I want to keep her there. That I could make her come like that so fast blows my mind. I know I've wanted her for what feels like forever. Has she ever wanted me before this moment?

Breaking the kiss first, I press my forehead to hers, trying to calm my accelerated breaths, my racing heart. I need to gain some control before I lose it. She opens her eyes, staring up at me, all sorts of questions in their hazel depths I can't begin to answer.

"Come home with me." The words fall from my lips before I can even stop them.

Her brows furrow. "What?"

"I want you to come home with me." I press my mouth to hers gently, inhaling her breath. I want more from her. I suddenly want it all from her.

And I have no right to ask for it.

"I don't know . . ." Her voice trails off when I press kisses to her jaw along her soft neck.

"Stay the night with me," I whisper against her throat. "Say yes, Ivy."

"Yes." The word falling so easily from her lips sends pleasure rippling through me. Lifting my head, I kiss her, drown in her like a starving man, telling myself I need to stop now before I lose all control and take her right here on the goddamn terrace.

"Jesus, Archer, you can't even keep your dick in your pants at a fucking wedding reception? What the hell is wrong with you?"

I let go of Ivy so fast at the sound of Gage's voice, I hear the click of her heels as she stumbles, though thank God she doesn't fall. Turning quickly, I face him, doing my best to compose myself. The way I'm standing hides Ivy completely and I wish like hell Gage hadn't found us.

"What are you doing out here?" I ask with a snarl,

feeling like an asshole. I shouldn't have let Ivy go like that. Like I'm ashamed to be seen with her.

More like she should be ashamed to be seen with me.

"Looking for you. And I was looking for Ivy. I see that you're preoccupied, though ..." Gage's voice trails off when he glances around my shoulder to see Ivy standing directly behind me. "What the fuck? Ivy, what are you doing out here with *him*?"

"Nothing," I say for the both of us. "She, uh ... she was having a bad night. I was trying to comfort her." Holy hell, what a choice of words.

Gage's frown is so fierce he looks like he wants to tear me apart. But his expression is also a mixture of doubt and disbelief. As if he can't believe the two of us are out here together. "Archer, I swear to God if you laid one finger on her ..."

"I didn't," I assure him, lying through my teeth. "I didn't touch her. Did I touch you, Ivy?"

She steps up so she's standing beside me, her body tense. Damn, I hope I didn't make her angry with my remark. "What did you ask?"

Shit. I did make her angry. She sounds furious.

"You better not have fallen for this dick's charms," Gage says, pointing his finger in Ivy's face. "You know how he is."

Lifting her chin, she glances at me out of the corner of her eye. "I know exactly how he is."

I now feel like a bug Ivy's ready to squash with her pointy heel. "Like I would mess with your sister, Gage. Come on. I'm not that stupid. I know you'd kick my ass if I so much as looked at Ivy the wrong way."

Gage stares at the both of us for long, quiet seconds. Seconds that feel like they stretch into hours, they're so uncomfortable. Doesn't help that Ivy is fuming mad. She practically has steam coming out of her ears, not that I can blame her.

I fucked up with her. Again.

What else is new?

Ivy

FOR A GROWN man who runs a multibillion dollar business, Archer Bancroft is a complete idiot when it comes to women.

My body was still shaking from the most amazing orgasm I'd ever experienced in my life when Gage stumbled upon us, giving Archer crap for fooling around with a woman on the terrace. Not that I blame my brother. It's such an Archer thing to do and here he is, doing it with me.

Shocking.

I hate to admit it, but Archer completely rocked my world. As in, no other man has ever made me come like that. Or come, period. I was ready to say yes to his asking me to come home with him. Passing up an opportunity to have sex with him after five amazing minutes with his fingers between my legs? I'm not stupid. I know sex with Archer would've been amazing. I came so fast, it's almost embarrassing.

Then Gage had to appear. And Archer had to open his mouth and completely ruin the entire moment.

I'm an idiot to think there could ever be anything real between us. Whatever just happened surely meant nothing to him. An opportunity to get with me—get with any woman really—and mess around for a few minutes. He's a known player.

And I just got played.

"I'm leaving soon," Gage finally says, his gaze falling on me. Since I came with him to this stupid wedding, I know what he's going to say next. "Are you ready to go, Ivy?"

"Yes." I nod and start toward my brother, barely withholding the gasp that wants to escape when Archer reaches for my hand, his fingers tangling with mine for the briefest second before they fall out of his grasp.

I glance over my shoulder and glare at him. He looks pitiful. Worried. Sorry.

Good. He should. Not that I care. I can't believe anything that just happened between us was sincere. I should be incredibly embarrassed at what happened between us. I fooled around with Archer. We almost got caught. Talk about a disaster waiting to happen.

"Call me Monday," Gage tells Archer as he rests his hand at my back, ready to guide me back toward the ballroom. "Let's do lunch this week. You're still coming to the city, right?"

"That's my plan." Archer's deep voice resonates within me, and I repress the shudder that wants to take over. I refuse to react in front of Archer. He doesn't need any more evidence that he affects me.

"Great. Let's definitely get together. See ya."

"Hey," Archer says softly and my brother and I both

still, though I refuse to turn around like Gage does. I don't even want to look at Archer, let alone talk to him. "Are you both headed back home tonight?"

"Well, yeah," Gage says with a shrug.

"You should stay the night at my place. It's not that far," Archer suggests, sounding innocent as all get out.

Gage glances at me and I glare back. Oh hell, no. I'm not staying the night at Archer's house. "I want to get home," I whisper.

"It's almost midnight," Gage whispers back. "We won't get back till past two, knowing traffic. I'm beat, Ive."

"I'll drive," I insist. "I'm wide awake. I can make it."

He raises a brow. "Like I'd let you drive my car. Give me break. You're a hazard behind the wheel."

I roll my eyes. One minor fender bender when I was seventeen and he never, ever lets me live it down. "I won't wreck, I swear."

"It's my Maserati. No way am I letting you drive it." Gage slowly shakes his head.

He wants to stay. I can tell by the look in his eyes. "Gage, no."

"I have plenty of bedrooms," Archer says, his voice hopeful.

I don't want to acknowledge him. Really, I don't. The more I think about what he did, the angrier I get. He said he would never touch me, all incredulous-like. As if he couldn't fathom me as anything but silly, gangly, awkward Ivy the teenage loser. What a jerk. After he just had his hand in my panties and begged me to stay the night with him . . .

Finally I chance a look at him. God, he's gorgeous. His suit is rumpled, his tie askew, his hair a mess. From my fingers. His lips are a little swollen and I remember how he kissed me, his taste, the sounds he made, the way he growled in my ear. Just like that I'm lightheaded and the feeling alone makes me want to slap myself back into reality.

Or maybe slap him for being so damn good at . . . everything.

Ugh.

"Come on," Gage says, nudging my side with his elbow. "We'll stay the night, grab brunch at that fancy hotel of his in the morning and then be on our way."

Hmm, I've never been to Hush. The chance to see it intrigues me but it shouldn't. Not after everything that's happened between us. "I have to get home. I have to . . . work."

"On a Sunday?" Gage sounds skeptical. Damn him. "Someone wants to have an emergency wallpaper meeting or what?"

Oh my God, I want to punch my brother so hard. I'd relish seeing him fall on his ass.

"Gage, shut the hell up. She probably does have to work," Archer says in my defense, which surprises me.

This is the guy who wanted me to come back to his place so he could get me naked in his bed. Maybe he has ulterior motives. Maybe he'll sneak into my room after Gage falls asleep and strip me and press me into the mattress and . . .

I frown, my hands tightening into fists. I shouldn't

want this. I shouldn't want him, especially after the way he spoke about me as if I don't matter to him.

But my body is singing a different song. As in, my skin is still humming after that amazing orgasm and my legs are a little shaky. Not from the stupid shoes with the four-inch heels either.

No, more like from the stupid man.

"Fine. We'll stay." I cross my arms in front of my chest. I probably look like a pouty baby but I don't really care. I can't believe I'm agreeing to this. "But we wake up, we grab brunch, and we get out of here. I really need to get back."

"Thanks, sis." Gage grabs my hand and brings it to his mouth, kissing the back of it quickly. "You just saved me from an exhausting drive home."

"Such a hardship since you're driving that precious car of yours." Cars are Gage's weakness. He owns too many of them. His addiction is so ridiculous his garage looks like an exclusive, high-end dealership.

"Glad you two are staying. I have guest rooms that are always prepared," Archer says.

I turn to glare at him once more, both uncomfortable and aroused at all the potential that comes with staying at his house. I'm sick in the head. I have to be to even consider . . . no, I can't go there. I blame the champagne. And the amazing orgasm. "You better be on your best behavior."

He throws up his hands in defense. "No funny business, I swear. I'll keep my hands to myself."

"You better, Bancroft, or I'll kick your ass," Gage mutters, his words backed with steel. "Ivy is hands-off when it comes to you."

"I get it," Archer says, slowly dropping his arms to his sides. The slight smirk falls from his face and his eyes meet mine, his gaze imploring. I'm not sure what he's trying to communicate, but I do know one thing.

When it comes to Archer and whatever's happening between us, I'm beyond confused.

Chapter Four

Ivy

HIS HOUSE IS amazing of course. I've been in plenty of beautiful homes in my life. My parents still reside in the palatial house Gage and I grew up in. It's older but large, and has all the warm, lived-in touches that our mom has added through the years. It's nothing compared to the modern, spacious, perfectly designed house Archer lives in in the heart of the Napa Valley.

Not that I can see much of it, considering the late hour. The interior is shrouded mostly in darkness, with only the occasional lamp turned on, but from what I can see it's beautiful. Sleek and simple, yet warm.

Archer leads Gage and me through the wide hallway toward the guest wing, as he calls it. One wall is made entirely of glass and I can make out a giant pool in the backyard, surrounded by lush, perfectly manicured landscaping that looks like something out of a park.

The man certainly knows how to live, I'll give him that.

"Nice, right?" Gage murmurs in my ear as we follow Archer. "I spend all my money on cars. Archer spends it all on his house."

"Not that I'm ever here," Archer says, revealing he spied on our conversation. No surprise. Since our encounter out on the terrace, I feel like he's hyperaware of me. And I'm hyperaware of him. "I spend most of my time at Hush."

"Do you have a room there?" The resort is treated as some sort of secret amongst my brother and his friends. At least, they keep it a secret from me. Always made me wonder if there are kinky secrets going down at that place.

Wouldn't put it past Archer, at least.

"I keep a suite there, yes." Archer slows so he can be closer to us. His scent reaches me, filling my head, reminding me of what it feels like to be wrapped in his arms, his broad shoulders beneath my palms. His hair is still a mess and he's shed the jacket and tie, the first couple of buttons on his shirt are undone and revealing a sliver of bare chest that I have the sudden urge to lick.

I really need to get a grip.

"So you stay at the resort most of the time?"

"Not as much as I used to. When it was being renovated I never left. I didn't even own a home then. Hush was my home. Now that the resort has been up and running for the last few years, I finally feel confident enough to leave it on occasion and actually have a life." Archer flashes me a smile, making my heart flutter.

Stupid heart.

"Hush is his baby," Gage adds like I don't know this, though it's fairly obvious. Considering Archer and I don't see each other much, let alone talk, it makes sense Gage would make that assumption. "He created it out of nothing but his own sick and twisted mind."

"Shut the hell up. I met a need that wasn't being filled. Pure and simple." Archer presses his lips together and his eyes narrow. He looks a little angry.

He also looks a lot sexy.

Stop!

"I'm intrigued. I'd love to see it," I say, pleased when his expression eases. "Maybe you'll take me on a quick tour of it tomorrow?"

"I thought you had to get right home tomorrow," Gage starts just before I jab him in the ribs with my elbow.

Yeah, Gage is right. But I'm curious to see this side of Archer's life that I know absolutely nothing about. I mean, come on. Not even an hour ago this man had his tongue down my throat and his fingers working me straight into oblivion. Any woman would want to know more about a guy after that sort of experience, right?

That's what I'm telling myself.

"I'd love to give you a tour of the resort," Archer says, his voice warm, his gaze hot as he rakes it over me. My skin ripples with awareness. It's as if he just physically touched me. "We'll have brunch and then I'll show you around."

"Sounds great." I smile, he returns it, and for some strange reason it feels like we're all alone, grinning at each other like idiots.

But then Gage clears his throat, bringing us both into reality, and I jolt at the sound, clasping my hands together to keep from reaching out and grabbing Archer.

I can't grab Archer, especially in front of my brother. No matter how badly I want to. Gage knows all of Archer's secrets, all of his faults. He loves his best friend, but Gage would never really want us together. At least, I don't think he would.

Better to pretend there's nothing between us rather than risk Gage's disapproval. And there's nothing going on with us. Between Archer and me. Really. A hot kiss and an orgasm. That's it.

That's sorta major.

I ignore the rotten little voice in my head and try to focus.

Regaining his composure, he shows us the guest rooms, which are directly across from each other, and I can't believe how beautiful my room is. The colors are soothing blues and grays, the bedding lush, the furniture dark and sleek. The entire room reeks of sophistication. I take it all in, fixating on the bed covered in plush fabrics since I'm so tired and I can't wait to collapse in it.

Or maybe the idea of Archer coming to this room later and making me come again and again is what really gets me going . . .

Overcome with a coughing attack at the thought, I wave Gage away when he shoots me a strange look. "I'm fine," I say as they both head toward the open doorway. "Show him his room, Archer. Good night."

Not giving either of them a chance to reply, I shut the door behind them and slump against it, thumping my head against the solid wood once, twice. Trying to knock sense into my brain, because clearly, I've lost it.

Sighing, I push away from the door and glance about the room, noting the open door that leads to a small connecting bathroom, and I go inside to check it out. All the amenities are here with the exception of what I might wear to bed. Not that I want to change into something left over from one of Archer's sexual conquests, but still. I'm surprised there's not a fresh, clean nightgown waiting for me to change into for the night, considering he has all the amenities. I guess I could wear my bra and panties . . .

Or wear nothing at all.

A little smile curling my lips, I find a plush terry cloth robe hanging from a hook on the back of the door. Running my hand over it, I contemplate taking a shower and start to shed my clothes, kicking off my shoes and letting the dress, my panties, and my bra fall into a pile on the floor.

I'll look like I'm doing the total night-after walk of shame tomorrow morning at Hush wearing the semiformal dress I wore to the wedding. Something I never considered until now and I chew on my lower lip, staring at the gigantic glass-enclosed shower calling my name.

Maybe I should ask Archer if he has something for me to wear. Though how do I approach him? Sure can't do it at the moment, since I'm standing here naked. He might not mind finding me this way, though.

Stop thinking like this. You don't want him to find you naked . . . do you?

Oh my God, maybe I do.

A knock sounds at the door and I jump, grabbing the robe off the hook with lightning speed. Throwing it on, I approach, figuring it's Gage ready to tell me something lame before he goes to bed. He's always been a little over-protective, so he's probably just checking up on me.

"I'm fine, Gage. Really," I say as I open the door, stunned silent when I see who's standing before me.

"Really?" Archer raises a brow, one hand in his pants' pocket, the other clutching an article of clothing. "Why wouldn't you be anything *but* fine?"

Oh. Shit. He should so not be standing in front of me right now. "What are you doing here?" I whisper, glancing over his shoulder to thankfully see Gage's door is closed.

"Making sure you're comfortable." He thrusts his hand out toward me. "I brought you something."

I'm ultra-aware of the fact that beneath the terry cloth, I'm wearing absolutely nothing. The impulse to untie the sash and let the robe drop to my feet just to see Archer's reaction is near overwhelming.

But I keep it under control. For now.

"What is this?" I take the wadded-up fabric from his hand, our fingers accidentally brushing, and heat rushes through me at first contact.

"One of my T-shirts." He shrugs those broad shoulders, which are still encased in fine white cotton. "I know you didn't have anything to wear to . . . bed. Thought I could offer you this."

His eyes darkened at the word *bed* and my knees wobble. Good lord, what this man is doing to me is so completely foreign, I'm not quite sure how to react.

"Um, thanks. I appreciate it." The T-shirt is soft, the fabric thin, as if it's been worn plenty of times, and I have the sudden urge to hold it to my nose and inhale. See if I can somehow smell his scent lingering in the fabric.

The man is clearly turning me into a freak of epic proportions.

"You're welcome." He leans his tall body against the doorframe, looking sleepy and rumpled and way too sexy for words. I want to grab his hand and yank him into my room.

Wait, no I don't. That's a bad—terrible—idea.

Liar.

"Is that all then?" I ask because we don't need to be standing here having this conversation. First, my brother could find us and start in again on what a mistake we are. Second, I'm growing increasingly uncomfortable with the fact that I'm completely naked beneath the robe. Third, I'm still contemplating shedding the robe and showing Archer just how naked I am.

"Yeah. Guess so." His voice is rough and he pushes away from the doorframe. "Well. Good night."

"Good night," I whisper, but I don't shut the door. I don't move.

Neither does he.

"Ivy . . ." His voice trails off and he clears his throat,

looking uncomfortable. Which is hot. Oh my God, everything he does is hot and I decide to give in to my impulses because screw it.

I want him.

Archer

LIKE AN IDIOT, I can't come up with anything to say. It's like my throat is clogged, and I can hardly force a sound out, what with Ivy standing before me, her long, wavy, dark hair tumbling past her shoulders, her slender body engulfed in the thick white robe I keep for guests. The very same type of robe we provide at Hush.

But then she does something so surprising—so amazingly awesome—I'm momentarily dumbfounded by the sight.

Her slender hands go for the belt of the robe and she undoes it quickly, the fabric parting, revealing bare skin. Completely bare skin.

Holy shit. She's naked. And she just dumped the robe onto the ground so she's standing in front of me. Again, I must stress, naked.

My mouth drops open, a rough sound coming from low in my throat. Damn, she's gorgeous. All long legs and curvy waist and hips and full breasts topped with pretty pink nipples. I'm completely entranced for a long, agonizing moment. All I can do is gape at her.

"Well, are you just going to stand there and wait for my brother to come back out and find us like this or are you going to come inside my room?"

More like I'm going to come inside her, if I'm lucky. Which I'm thinking I'm gonna be.

Moving fast, I crowd her, my hands going to her waist as I push her inside. I kick the door shut, snaking out a hand behind me to turn the lock before I settle it back on her waist.

The mention of Gage finding us like this got me moving. He'd tear my balls off with his bare hands if he knew I was touching his sister at this very moment. And then there's that whole stupid bet I just made with him and Matt. Here I went on and on about not letting any chick tie me down and the one woman I secretly consider worth having a relationship with is finally showing a glimmer of interest.

Well, more than a freaking glimmer considering she's naked and nestling that bangin' body all snug up against me. I stare into her eyes, see them clouded with lust, and I lean in ready to kiss her. To take her deep and hard and make her moan with the pleasure of it all. Just like I did earlier, when I touched her out on the terrace. How easily responsive she'd been. Before I ruined it all and blew off what happened between us. Last thing I wanted was to make her angry, but I still managed, all because I didn't want to piss off Gage.

I'm in a total no-win situation with Ivy and I know it. Yet here I am, her naked body in my arms, her lips leaning in close to mine, her breasts coming into contact with my chest . . .

"Hey." I squeeze her hips, my fingers pressing into her flesh, and she glances up at me, her eyes wide, her lips damp. As if she'd just licked them. Fuck, everything she does unravels me. But I need to know where we stand—where she stands. I can't risk making this a bigger mess than it already is. "What are we doing here?"

A perfectly arched brow lifts. "Do I need to explain it to you?"

"You know what I mean." I'm not taking this any further until I'm assured we're both on the same page. "What do you want out of this?"

Ivy reaches out and starts unbuttoning my shirt, her fingertips brushing against my chest with every button she slides out of its hole. "One night of mind-blowing sex?"

I ignore the one-night comment for a moment, absorbing her words. I shouldn't want more. I never want more.

With Ivy, I think I could.

Well, isn't that fucking terrifying?

"And that's it." My voice is flat, though I suck in a harsh breath when her fingers brush my stomach with that final button she undoes before tugging my tucked-in shirt from the waistband of my pants. "That's all you want from me."

"Isn't that all you want from anyone?" Her gaze locks on my chest and she exhales loudly. "I knew you were bigger than the last time I saw you, Archer, but oh my God."

I smile, loving the way she's looking at me. Like she wants to eat me up. "And when was the last time you saw me without a shirt on?"

"I don't know." She shrugs, her gaze lifting to meet mine. Her eyes are full of hunger, full of want, and I reach out, settle my hand on her cheek, and caress her soft skin. It's like I can't resist touching her. "When we were teenagers?"

"Well, I've changed a lot since then." Leaning down, my mouth is at her ear when I murmur, "So have you."

She slides her hands up my chest, her touch causing sparks to ignite along my skin as she pushes my shirt from my shoulders. I shrug out of it, settling my hands back at her waist, pulling away a bit so I can drink her in.

Jesus, she's gorgeous. I'm hard as a rock just looking at her and I start to back her toward the bed, pushing gently at her shoulders so she falls onto the mattress with a little huff of annoyance. Her long hair falls around her shoulders in tousled waves, the ends barely covering her breasts, tempting me to rake my fingers through the silky strands. Without warning she hooks her finger through the belt loop of my pants, pulling me forward and tipping me off balance so I fall onto the bed.

Fall onto her.

"Now I have you where I want you," she murmurs just before she lifts her head and kisses me deep, her tongue immediately sliding against mine. She skims her hands down my back so lightly I shiver.

Damn, her touch feels good. She feels good beneath me, her hands on me, her legs winding around my hips. I still have my pants on but I can feel her. My erection nudges against her heated sex and she tilts her hips, grinding against me as she devours my mouth.

She's turned into a wildcat, rubbing against me, her mouth on mine like she wants to consume me and I willingly fall under her spell. Let her take completely over, as I'm lost to her delicious taste, the way her tiny hands are all over me, at the front of my pants. Undoing the snap, sliding the zipper down until she's reaching inside and stroking my cotton-covered cock.

"Wow, Archer, you're packing," she murmurs after breaking our kiss, her fingers curling around my erection and giving me an agonizing squeeze.

I burst out laughing at her comment. "Is that supposed to be a compliment?"

"Oh yeah." She slides her hands around my hips, pushing my pants down until they bunch up about mid-thigh. "Take these off. Take everything off."

"Bossy little thing, aren't you?" I whisper against her mouth just before I swipe at her plump lower lip with my tongue.

"I never act like this," she says when I climb off her to shed the rest of my clothes. Her greedy gaze never leaves me. "I think it's all your fault."

"My fault?" Her admission shocks me. How can she blame me for her crazy behavior? "How so?"

"It's you or the champagne I drank earlier." Her gaze drops to crotch level and she's checking me out, her eyes widening the slightest bit once I shed my boxer briefs. "Um, wow."

"Scared?" I rejoin her on the bed, grabbing her by the waist and hauling her over until she's lying beneath me. "You should be," I whisper before I kiss her. Devour her. It grows wild in an instant, my hands roaming her skin, mapping her curves, her hands just as busy as mine, diving straight for my cock. I'll blow if she keeps touching me like that, and I'm not about to go that route, so I grasp hold of her wrists and pull her arms up above her head. Holding her captive and she wiggles against me, making little noises full of frustration.

Driving me fucking insane.

She breaks the kiss first, glaring at me as she jerks her hands against my grip. "I want to touch you."

"You keep on touching me and I'm going to explode all over your fingers," I growl.

Ivy laughs, arching against me so her breasts brush my chest. I can literally feel the hard points of her nipples press into my skin.

This woman is going to kill me. I just know it.

Chapter Five

Ivy

ARCHER BANCROFT HAS a body like no other man I've been with before, let alone seen live and in person, up close and in my face. All solid mass and smooth skin, defined muscles and broad chest and shoulders. He's all I can see and hear and smell and taste while he lies on top of me, his long fingers curled around my wrists, holding my arms captive above my head.

What we're doing is so completely unexpected, so unbelievably exciting, my entire body is shaking in anticipation. He's kissing me like he's a starving man and I'm the only thing he craves. I can feel his erection nudging between my legs, and I'm so wet for him it's almost embarrassing.

But I don't care. I'm drunk on the sensation of his body pressing into mine, his hungry mouth, his insistent tongue, those big, rough hands pinning me to the bed.

I had no idea being held down would arouse me so much, but oh my God, I'm so hot for him I feel like I'm going to burst.

"Promise not to go straight for my dick?" he whispers in my ear after breaking our kiss.

I want to laugh. I also want to moan. His blunt words turn me on too. "Maybe I really want to go straight for your dick."

His eyes lock with mine. They're dark and full of smoldering heat. "I already told you what might happen if you did that."

Oh yes, he sure did. I might want to witness that too. In fact, the idea is amazingly hot. Me stroking him, Archer losing all control and coming all over my fingers . . .

Restlessly I rub my legs against his, and he chuckles as if he can read my mind. "Promise me you won't make a grab."

"I can't promise you that," I whisper.

"Then let me touch you." His voice lowers as his fingers loosen gently around my wrists. Until they're slipping away and he's nuzzling my neck with his face, his hands skimming along my sides. "I want to explore you."

I'm not going to protest. That's exactly what I want him to do. So instead of making a grab for his dick—as he so kindly says—I sling my arms around his neck, my hands in his hair, gently guiding him down as he rains kisses across my collarbone, my chest, the tops of my breasts, the valley between my breasts . . .

He's teasing me. My nipples ache for his mouth to wrap around them and his lips are everywhere but my nipples. I don't know if I can stand this exquisite torture, his hands gripping my hips, his mouth all over my sensitive skin. I tighten my hold on his hair, tugging hard until he mutters a curse word against my flesh before he licks one nipple.

Then he licks the other.

The ragged moan that escapes me is nothing like the usual sounds I make in bed, and I clamp my lips shut, momentarily embarrassed. But then he does it again, his velvety damp tongue flicking back and forth over my nipple, driving me absolutely wild. Another shuddery moan leaves me, and I tangle my fingers in his hair, holding him to me as he licks and sucks and edges his teeth on my flesh, gently nipping. Testing me.

It feels so good I want more. Oh God, I'm crazed with wanting his teeth on me, his hands all over me. "Harder," I whisper, my request shocking myself and he bites my nipple, hard.

Between my legs I go loose and damp and when he glides his fingers through my soaked folds, his thumb sweeping over my clit, I shake my head frantically. "No, not like this. Please."

"Want me inside you?" He whispers the heated words against my breasts, and I crack open my eyes to find him watching me. His gaze is dark, full of forbidden promise, and I nod, a whimper falling from my lips. His answering smile is deliciously wicked. "Good. Because I can't fucking wait to be inside you."

No man has ever talked to me like this. I love it. I want more. So much more . . .

Moving up, he leans over me, his chest in my face as he reaches for the bedside table and pulls open the tiny drawer. He withdraws a condom from inside, and I'm momentarily stunned.

Though I shouldn't be. Everyone knows how Archer operates.

Pushing the worry from my head, I lean up on my elbows and press my mouth to the center of his chest. His scent surrounds me, the warmth of his skin, his salty taste. I'm licking a path down to his abs and he pulls away from me, hissing as if I've burned him.

"You're dangerous," he murmurs, tearing open the wrapper and rolling on the condom. The sight of him entrances me and my heart rate accelerates, my mouth going dry when he catches me staring. He shakes his head with a slight smile curving his perfect, swollen lips. "I want to take my time but I doubt I'll make it, Ivy. I want you too damn much."

Again, he stuns me, this time with his words. If I think about it too hard, the entire situation is mind blowing. I'm naked with Archer Bancroft. We're about to have sex. If someone told me a month ago—heck, a few hours ago—that I would end this night having sex with Archer, I would've laughed in their face.

I'm not laughing now, though. More like I'm grabbing for Archer, bringing him down on top of me, his big body pushing me into the mattress. I wrap my legs around his hips, curl my arms around him so I can stroke down his smooth, damp-with-sweat back as our mouths find each other, lazily kissing, nipping at each other's lips, tangling our tongues.

He tastes amazing. I love the sounds he makes, the way he holds me. And when he slowly slides inside my body, inch by excruciating inch, a shudder sweeps over me, my eyes shutting against the intensity of emotions swirling within. He doesn't move, doesn't so much as breathe, and I'm breathless too. I've never felt so connected to another person before.

It's frightening. Exhilarating.

"Christ, you feel so good," he whispers close to my ear as he slowly begins to move. I shift with him, lifting my hips, tightening my legs around him. He's thrusting faster, almost as if he can't help himself, and I'm fine with it. More than fine with it. I rock against him, sending his cock deeper inside my body, and he's groaning, straining above me, already close. I can see it in the tension in his face, across his shoulders.

He warned me it would be fast but I don't care. I'm close too. I've been on edge since he made me come on the terrace. There'd been no relief with that orgasm. More like it ratcheted me up, helping me realize what I was missing, not being with him like this.

"Say you're going to come," he whispers, his ragged voice sending a shiver over my skin. "Say it." He reaches between us, his fingers slipping over my clit, rubbing circles around it, driving me straight out of my mind.

"Yes," I moan. "So close."

Archer rears up on his knees and grasps hold of my waist, pulling me closer as he pounds into me. I watch, breathless at the brutal way he's handling me, truly fucking me, and I wonder if any man I've ever been with has done this. Fucked me like Archer is at this very moment.

That would be a firm no.

The men of my past always handled me gently, as if I were made of glass and might shatter at any moment. Not Archer. He's all macho, primal fierceness, his hands gripping me, his cock pounding inside of me, his mouth brutalizing mine. It's as if he's completely overcome.

I love it.

Closing my eyes, the familiar sensations threaten to wash over me, and I try to hold them off. Whimpering, I shake my head, pant his name and then I can't hold back any longer.

I'm coming. Lost in the deliciously warm pulsating sensation as the second orgasm of the night takes me completely over the edge.

He collapses on top of me seconds later, his warm weight comforting, yet making it all feel far too real. His mouth presses to my neck, wet and hot as he whispers unintelligible words. I smooth my fingers down his back, feel the shivers still trembling through him, and I kiss his cheek, murmuring, "You should probably go soon." I wince the moment the words leave my mouth. I really don't want him to leave.

But he needs to. If he lingers . . . I might want him

to stick around. Then I might do something stupid. Like admit how much I care for him, how much I wish he were a permanent part of my life.

Yeah. He'd flip out and run like a scared little boy if I ever said something like that.

Lifting up so he can meet my gaze, he studies me, his brows furrowed, his mouth curved in a frown. "What?"

Uh oh. Did I say the wrong thing? Come on, Archer isn't one who lingers in a woman's bed, is he? "You um, you should probably go, don't you think? I don't want my brother to see you sneak out of my room."

"He's probably asleep. That guy sleeps like the dead." Archer's studying me like I've lost my mind.

"Yeah, but . . ." He's right I'm sure. I don't want to risk the chance. Besides, I need time alone. I need to process what just happened between us.

"So you're kicking me out." He sounds incredulous, looks angry.

"No . . ."

"Yes," he cuts me off, his voice tight. "I get it, though. Don't want Gage to find out. I agree with you, actually. He'll hang me by my balls from a tree, and I happen to like my balls, thank you very much."

He climbs out of bed, snatching his clothes off the floor impatiently, giving me an unintended eyeful of those very balls he happens to like so much.

Crap, I've made him mad. I didn't mean to but I can't have him lingering. It's bad enough what we just did. I don't do one-night stands, especially with guys I know and run the risk of seeing again. Worse, I don't want to get attached. Or put expectations on us that this sort of thing might happen again.

Because no way should it happen again. That would be a big mistake. Huge. No more fooling around for Archer and me.

Even though I want to. I hate that I'm pushing him away. His reaction is confusing. He acts like he's hurt by my denial.

I'm hurt too. More than I would ever dare admit. Deep down inside, I think . . . I want more. For once, I'm ready to take that risk and go for it. Do something so completely out of character just to see what would happen.

"You still want to see Hush later today?" he asks, his voice quiet, his back to me. He has on his underwear, nothing else, and I let my gaze wander over him, drinking in all that pure masculine beauty.

He *is* beautiful. I wish we had more time. I'd explore every inch of his skin with my mouth, given the chance.

Your chances with Archer just expired.

"Yes," I answer after I clear my throat. "I would love to see Hush." We can handle a mistaken sexual encounter between friends, right? Of course we can . . .

"Great. Well, it's been real," he says after he slips on his pants, still sounding sort of huffy, and I watch him go without saying another word. He quietly shuts the door behind him.

I flop against the pillows and rest my arm over my eyes, groaning out loud. What the heck is wrong with me? I had amazing sex with a man I've known almost half my life, and then I push him out like he's some sort of stranger I secretly banged.

I can't help it. I start laughing.

My life has turned completely surreal.

Archer

DAMN, COULD I feel any cheaper?

I'm skulking down the hall of my very own home, shirtless and shoeless, my clothes and shoes clutched in my hand, my pants unbuttoned, for the love of God, and ready to fall from my hips. My footsteps are light as I'm literally sprinting across my house. If Gage came out at this very moment, he would take one look at me and know exactly what I'd just done.

His baby sister.

Grimacing, I shake my head and head toward my bedroom suite, which is on the other side of the house. I'm breathing a little easier now that I'm out of the guest wing, but I could still get caught. That I'm even thinking like this makes me feel like an absolute jackass.

This is my house. I'm twenty-fucking-eight years old. I shouldn't have to sneak around like some sort of teenager out screwing around with my secret girlfriend.

But here I am. Sneaking.

I'm still shocked over how Ivy kicked me out of bed before the come dried on her skin; she was that ruthless about the entire encounter. Crude, I know, but true. I'd been ready to wax poetic and go on and on over how amazing that entire experience had been. Because as quick as I'd come—embarrassingly quick, I'll admit, but damn I was overwhelmed with the fact that I was actually inside her—sex with Ivy had been mind blowing.

I wanted to tell her how much I wanted to do it again. Clutch her close and cuddle for Christ's sake. I don't fucking cuddle. I'm the one who kicks them out of my bed. I'm the one who says, *Hey, it's been real, but you need to get your pretty little ass out of here.*

Always, I sleep alone. For once, I wanted to sleep with someone else. Really and truly sleep. Hold her close, feel her skin on mine, smell her. I can still smell her. Feel her. Taste her.

She gave me the boot instead.

Yeah. Bizarre. I feel like the tables have been turned on me completely. I don't like it. Not one freaking bit.

But since I saw her earlier this evening at the wedding reception, she's flipped me on my head. What's up is down and all that other bullshit. I haven't felt right since. It fucking sucks. I have a business to run, employees to take care of, the potential to open another Hush location on the horizon and a volatile father to handle.

The last thing I need is some woman twisting up my insides.

I stride inside my bedroom, slamming the door behind me and head toward the bathroom. I need a shower. Maybe if I wash away the memory, the feel of her skin on mine, her scent, her taste, then I could forget her. Ivy.

Doesn't help. As I stand under the scalding hot water battering my body and scrub at my skin, I can still smell her. Hear her panting, frantic breaths, the way she said my name just before she came. Smell her flowery, delicious skin, taste her greedy lips and tongue . . .

Fuck. I glance down, the water beating a rapid tattoo on the top of my head, and see my erection. Fucking stupid thing. No wonder women loved to go on and on about how men only think with their dicks.

They're pretty dead on in that observation.

Restraining myself, I refuse to jerk off. I just came not fifteen minutes ago, you'd think I'd be over this. Over her.

Apparently not. Having her once wasn't enough. I want Ivy again.

I furiously wrench the faucet off and grab a towel, rubbing it haphazardly across my skin, not really drying it. The soft terry cloth slides across my erection and I grimace. Pissed that I'm teasing myself. What the hell is wrong with me?

Ivy Emerson is what's wrong with you, jackass. She's played you at your game and actually came out on top. Where does that leave you?

Miserable. Pissed. Eager to go back to her room and have my way with her again . . . slower this time. So I can linger over her body, see what she likes, where she prefers to be touched, taste her between her legs and see how long it takes to make her come with just my tongue . . .

Rubbing the heels of my hands against my eyes, I blink them open, stare at my reflection in the steam-covered mirror in front of me. I'm a wreck. Eyes wild, skin still wet from the shower, mouth and jaw so tight I look like I might shatter. Rigid and tense.

All over a woman.

I let loose a loud, growling "Fuck!" and hit the lights off, stride back into my room. Climb into bed naked and still damp, yanking the covers over my head in the hopes I can shut off my whirling brain.

Doesn't work. I want her with me. Snug against me. I need to come clean with myself. I've lusted over her for years. Since her high school graduation, like some sort of pervert, considering I have a solid four years on her and the last thing I should've been doing was wondering if she could possibly be naked beneath her ceremony gown.

Of course, she wasn't. She'd been eighteen and pure and beautiful. She'd given me a hug and thanked me for coming and all I could think about was how much I wish I *was* coming. Inside of her . . .

Yeah. I had it bad for her then. I still do. And I shouldn't. I'm not the relationship type. My parents warped me for good. Ruined me for any woman. I might be able to hold my shit together for a while, but she'd wear me down eventually and discover the real me.

I'm not worth it, not worth making it last. I'm selfish. A complete prick. She'd find out quickly, if she doesn't know already, and she'd bail. Wonder why she wasted her time on me, if she'd even consider me, that is.

And then there's that stupid, fucked-up bet I made only a few hours ago. A million dollars rides on the idea that I won't let any woman trap me.

The crazy thing? I know Ivy Emerson is worth a million dollars.

But am I?

Chapter Six

Ivy

SOMEHOW, ARCHER ARRANGED for a fresh set of clothes to be waiting for me when I opened my bedroom door earlier. They sat in a neat, folded pile, tucked in a bag that was set in front of my door. A pair of black cotton cropped pants, a bright pink T-shirt, and a pair of my favorite brand of flip-flops. All in the proper sizes, all of it cute and something I would probably pick out on my own if given the chance.

How the hell did he know my sizes? Sorta scary.

I never heard anyone pass by the door either. And I would've. I tossed and turned, hardly getting any sleep, what with my thoughts consumed by what happened between Archer and me.

Images had flashed all night. The way he looked at me. How he touched me. The things he said to me.

I can't fucking wait to be inside you.

God, I melt just remembering how dark his voice had sounded, the way he whispered those words close to my ear, his hands all over my body.

A shudder moves through me and I let loose a frustrated huff, then proceed to take a long shower in the hopes the hot water would wash away all of my useless and overwhelming feelings for a man I have no business feeling anything over.

Unfortunately, it didn't work. Considering I'm in Archer's house after being in his arms the night before, he permeates everything.

I both secretly love it and openly hate it.

I get dressed quickly, pulling my wet hair into a low ponytail with a band I found in the bottom of my purse. Slicked on some lip gloss because that's all the makeup I brought with me.

No one's called me, no Gage, no Archer. No one has even knocked on my door, and finally curiosity gets the better of me. I open the door and peek my head out, glancing left, then right, but the hall is empty. Gage's door is closed. The house is quiet; it's like I'm staying in a museum or something and I step fully out of the room, contemplating going to knock on Gage's door.

What if he's still sleeping? It's already past nine and Gage isn't one to sleep in. Deciding I need to know what's up, I approach the door and knock, stumped when he doesn't answer. No way can he still be in bed. And if he is, what a total bum.

"He's outside, waiting for you."

I jump and turn at the sound of Archer's deep voice,

surprised to find him standing in the middle of the vast hallway. Like a ghost, he magically appeared. And what a good-looking ghost he is too. He's dressed in jeans and a black polo shirt, his dark hair is still damp, as if he just came out of the shower and oh wow, he looks amazing. I'm filled with the urge to take him by the hand, drag him back into my bedroom, and strip him. Run my hands all over his delicious body. Ride him into oblivion.

Stop!

"Oh." I can't come up with anything better to say so I don't. Ridiculous how I thought a little sex between two age-old friends—acquaintances, really—would be no big deal, but it's like the giant elephant filling the entire house, sitting directly between us. I meet his gaze and all I can do is remember how close his face had been to mine a few hours ago as he thrust deep inside my body. How I craned my neck and met his mouth with mine, our tongues sliding against each other's.

Yeah. This is . . . awkward.

"We're leaving for Hush soon. Are you ready?" His velvety smooth voice sends shivers running over my skin, and I press my lips together, searching for composure.

So far, I can't really find it.

"I need to grab my purse." I gesture toward the open door, then let my hand fall helplessly at my side.

"Did you sleep all right?" His question is innocent and courteous considering I'm his guest. But he mentions sleep, which makes me think of a bed, and then I'm remembering how he was in my bed and how fantastic he felt between my legs.

"I slept fine. Great," I lied. "Um, thank you for the clothes."

"You're welcome. You like them?"

"They're . . . perfect." I frown and he does as well. "How did you know my sizes?"

"I took a wild guess." He said this with a shrug, looking a little sheepish. This of course makes me skeptical. Just goes to show how well Archer knows his way around the female body when he can guess my size accurately.

My gut clenches at the realization.

"Oh." I'm at a complete loss of words. His explanation makes perfect sense. Our being together makes absolutely no sense. Clearly, we made a huge mistake. And now we're paying the price with the awkward silences and uncomfortable vibe between us.

"I'll get my purse and then I'll be ready."

"Meet us out front then?" He smiles at me but it's grim. And it doesn't quite light up his eyes.

"Yes. Give me just a second." I nod once, shooting into the bedroom the second he turns away from me.

Going to the bed, I sit on the edge heavily, chewing on my thumbnail as I give myself a mental pep talk.

You can handle this. So you've seen him naked. So what? And you know what he looks like when he comes. Big deal. Focus on the old days. When he used to be such a jerk to you and treated you so terribly. Remember how you felt last night at the reception, when he first talked to you and called you "chicken." Jerk. Yeah, he irritated the crap out of you. Hold on to that feeling. The Archer Bancroft-drives-me-out-of-my-mind-he's-such-an-asshole feeling.

Forget all about the Archer Bancroft-drives-me-out-of-my-mind-when-he's-kissing-me-senseless-and-fucking-me-into-oblivion feeling. That is so the wrong feeling to hold on to.

Picking up my purse, which I left on the bed, I stand, tug at the hem of my new, cute T-shirt, smooth a hand over my hair, and decide to go face my reality.

I can handle this. Because really, I don't have a choice.

Archer

"WHAT THE HELL is taking her so long? I'm starved."

"Grumpy bastard," I mutter, irritated with Gage's incessant miserable chatter. He hasn't quit griping about his empty stomach since the moment I ran into him in the kitchen. I offered him an apple but he wouldn't take it. Heaven forbid he eats something healthy. And besides, it's not my fault his sister is taking so long to get ready.

Why, I'm not sure. I saw her no more than five minutes ago, looking absolutely gorgeous in the simple outfit I left for her to change into. I'd been half tempted to grab her by the waist, walk her backward into the bedroom, lock the door, and have my way with her for the rest of the day. Talk about an ideal lazy Sunday.

But I knew Gage was waiting and besides, the panicked expression on her face when she first saw me deflated my ego completely. She looked ready to jump and run.

Did she regret what happened between us last night? I don't, but I gotta admit, the vibe between us just now was uncomfortable yet hyperaware.

Were we going to pretend it never happened? That was probably best: act like what we shared last night was some sort of weird—and fucking amazing—dream. Acknowledging it the morning after only asked for trouble, especially since Gage was present.

A grumbling, moody Gage. He's acting like a bear you'd regret poking too hard.

"You need coffee or what? I told you there's a freshly made pot in the kitchen," I say, unable to stand his moodiness one second longer.

"Bah." Gage waves a hand. "I've had your coffee before. It's complete shit."

I don't bother reminding him that I had the housekeeper make a fresh pot of coffee every morning. Just one of the many perks of having a lot of money. Gage is still stuck on us being college roommates when I used to make coffee that tasted like black oil sludge.

"Whatever. You're missing out." I glance toward the door, standing up straight when it opens, revealing Ivy, who stops on the top step. She's looking fresh as a damn daisy, her hair still wet from the shower and pulled into a ponytail, showcasing that pretty face of hers. Her eyes sparkle, her cheeks are flushed, and when she catches sight of the both of us standing in front of my Mercedes, a smile curls those sensuous lips. Lips I tasted again and again last night.

Lips I'd like to see curled around my . . .

I frown. Damn it, I really need to stop thinking about her like that.

Her smile fades just as quick as it appeared. Like she

caught herself doing it and realized her mistake. Or she noticed my frown.

Hell.

"Finally," Gage calls out. "Let's get going before they stop serving brunch."

"They serve it until two," I mutter, wishing like crazy Gage wasn't with us. Of course, if he wasn't, we wouldn't be going to Hush either, and I'm excited to show off my baby to Ivy.

"I forgot what a grump you are in the morning until you get some food in your stomach." She approaches us, her eyes soft when they light on me. "Sorry to keep you waiting."

"You're right on time," I assure her, because at this very moment she really can do no wrong.

"I call shotgun," Gage says as he reaches for the passenger-side door handle.

I slap my hand against the door, stopping him from opening it. "Are you so freaking hungry that you lost your mind? Let your sister sit in the front."

"Why?" Gage sounds boggled. And clueless.

I should be thankful for clueless. If he was feeling a little sharper this morning, he might catch on to the weirdness going on between Ivy and me.

"Stop being such an infant and just sit in the back seat." I jerk my thumb toward the back of the car.

"I can sit in the back . . ." Ivy starts, but I shake my head, cutting her off.

"Sit in the front." I say it like a command, which gets those perfectly arched eyebrows of hers rising, and I round the front of the car without another word, sliding behind the steering wheel and starting the car.

I don't mean to be such a bossy ass but Gage is on my last damn nerve.

She slides into the passenger seat, sitting right beside me, her usual floral scent not as strong. I can only assume that's because she didn't use her own products. Shampoo, body wash, perfume . . . I wish I knew exactly what made her smell so good. Perhaps it's a mixture of everything, plus her own unique scent.

"It's a beautiful morning," Ivy says, her head turned away from me, nose practically pressed against the glass of the window. "I wouldn't be able to get any work done if I had this sort of view distracting me every day."

I pull out of the driveway, taking in my surroundings, ignoring the snort that emanates from the back seat. I thought I turned into an adolescent when I got near Ivy. Gage was ten times worse, switching to jerk big brother mode within seconds of Ivy making an appearance.

"After living here for so many years, I don't even notice it," I say, turning left and heading toward Hush. The resort is not far from my house, so the drive is easy. Beautiful.

Definitely beautiful, not that I'd noticed it much. Too distracted with work, too distracted with the business opportunity that suddenly came up. Thankfully, it's an opportunity that will keep me in Napa Valley, but I know my father worries it might be a mistake, working on a new venture so close to the already successful Hush resort. Why mess with a good thing, is basically what he told me.

Not for the first time in our lives, I completely disagree with him. I know what I'm doing. So I screwed around in college and didn't get the best grades—so what? I might've spent more time chasing women and going to parties versus studying and actually attending classes, but guess what? I got my education in the real world. Growing up in the Bancroft Hotels gave me the hands-on experience and vision needed to take the company to the next level.

Too bad my father didn't realize it.

"Do you miss the city?" Ivy asks, knocking me from my thoughts.

I glance over to find her studying me. "Sometimes. Not that it's far, but I haven't had much time lately to make it over. Not as if I want to visit my parents . . . I like the pace here, though. It's a little slower. More reflective."

"Are you trying to say you're reflective?" Gage pipes up from the back seat. "Give me a break."

I press my lips together to keep from calling Gage an insensitive prick.

"Ignore him," Ivy whispers, reaching over to pat my thigh. "He's just jealous."

"Yeah, right," Gage laughs, but I don't reply.

I'm too caught up in the fact that she touched my thigh, and just like that I'm sporting a hard-on. A full-blown one too, all from a light touch of her fingers on my leg.

This is . . . bad. If I can barely handle her touching me on the leg for a brief second, then I need to get her out of my life pronto.

Or pull her so deeply into my life there's no way she'd ever want to leave my side again.

Keep dreaming, asshole.

Funny how the nagging voice inside my head sounds just like Gage.

Chapter Seven

Ivy

THE RESORT IS gorgeous. Unlike anything I've ever seen, and I've been to more than a few exclusive spas and resorts in my life. My mom loves to indulge in spas and she's taken me on many a "girls only" trip the last few years. She's all about the detox.

But the Hush Resort is more than just a simple spa. And it's definitely more than a hotel too. From what I can see since Archer's taken us on a tour of the lush grounds, it's all about promoting a lifestyle.

Indulgence. Decadence. Sex. That's the message Hush is sending me, albeit in a sophisticated, understated package. I noticed from the moment we were seated in the small on-premise restaurant we're surrounded by couples. Young, old, middle-aged, every one of them is so in tune with each other, so focused and seemingly happy, I can't help but admire each and every one of them.

And also feel a little jealous.

I sat with two men, the lone oddity in the entire restaurant. One is my jerk of a brother who can't quite stop giving Archer grief while stuffing his face. I have no idea what's gotten into Gage but it isn't a pleasant sight.

Then there's Archer, who's been quiet since we arrived. He seems almost . . . nervous, and I've never seen Archer nervous. Of course, I'd never seen Archer naked either, but I sure remedied that last night now, didn't I?

I feel like I'm seeing all the bits and pieces that make him up. It's rather fascinating, though I tell myself I most definitely should not be fascinated. What happened between us was a mistake. Why I can't seem to remember that, I'm not exactly sure.

Hormonal issues maybe? Yes, that must be it.

After breakfast, he takes us for a tour, showing us the gorgeously landscaped grounds with what seems like miles of lush green grass spread around the facility. The rolling hills that surround the hotel location are dotted with the vineyards' neat rows and my eyes are constantly drawn to their simple, efficient beauty. The day is crisp and clear, the sky a startling blue, the sun warm on my skin, and I glance around in utter amazement, overwhelmed with all the natural beauty that's surrounding me.

"You like it?" Archer asks, sounding eager.

"I do." I smile up at him, unable to contain it. I don't want to give him any wrong ideas, but wow, I'm blown away with his resort. "The location is unreal."

"My father bought the property years ago, before I was even born," Archer explains, his gaze going to the vineyards, just like mine does. "The old Bancroft Hotel in Napa that's not too far slowly turned into a complete loser, a financial drain. Couldn't turn a profit, was considered in a less-than-ideal location."

"I'm surprised," I say, interrupting him. He turns to look at me, his eyebrows raised, and I shrug. "Just the beauty of the location alone is breathtaking. And you haven't taken us inside any of the buildings yet besides the restaurant. I'm sure I'll become even more impressed."

Gage wanders off, seemingly bored with the conversation, but I'm sure he's heard it all before. Funny, how Archer and I have never spent any sort of time alone together like this. Until now.

"Well, I had the original hotel building razed when my father sent me out here. I started over completely from scratch. And when I say it wasn't an ideal location, it's because so many other hotels were built in another, much more populated area. This one was considered out of the way." He slips his hands into the front pockets of his jeans, looking so gorgeous as the breeze ruffles his dark hair I want to lunge at him. Grab hold and never let go.

I keep myself in check instead.

"You've done an amazing job," I say softly. "You must be proud."

"Yeah, I am." He smiles, his eyes warm. "It wasn't easy. My father sent me out here to fail."

I frown. "He did?"

"Of course he did. He had no faith in me. I was a

world-class screwup, I'll admit it. I didn't want to work, not directly for him, at least. So he said since I thought I knew what the hell I was doing, he'd give me this." Archer's smile turned rueful. "I showed him, didn't I?"

"How long ago was that?" I knew his relationship with his father wasn't the best, but to send his son out to purposely fail with a bad location? Awful.

"Over three years ago. Construction took a solid ten months to a year and we opened when only a few buildings were completed, expanding as each one was finished. Hush made Bancroft a lot of money in the first six months it was open." He studies the vineyards in the near distance, his expression serious, not the usual smiling, charming Archer.

My heart aches for him, no matter how much I tell it to stop.

I'm impressed with his success story. I remember how it was when we were younger. His dad constantly disappointed in him. His mother never around, or always drunk and crying over the way her husband treated her. No wonder Archer spent all of his time at our house when he and Gage became such good friends. My parents weren't perfect, but at least they get along for the most part and they have a relatively normal relationship.

No drunken yelling or icy-cold neglect.

"Such a great story," I say, wincing the moment the words fall from my lips. More like such a lame comment for a truly amazing accomplishment.

"Yeah, well, tell that to my father." His voice is tight, as is his jaw.

I hate that he feels this way. He should be proud of what he's done in such a short amount of time, versus fixated on his father's shoddy treatment of him over the years.

"Is this hotel part of the Bancroft chain or is it separate?" I'm not quite sure why I'm asking him this, but I have to know.

"It's all mine. He signed it over to me." He turns to look at me. "I told you he thought I would fail. He had no problem giving it to me figuring I would lose my ass over it."

The pain in his voice is undeniable. "You certainly proved him wrong," I say softly.

"Sure as hell did." His gaze meets mine, dark and mysterious, his mouth grim. My heart flutters and I step toward him. Somehow wanting to offer him comfort, solace, something. Anything. He's hurting and it makes me hurt for him.

"What made you decide to create a resort like Hush in the first place?" I'm desperate to change the subject. The last thing he ever wants to talk about is his dad or his mom.

"I knew it would turn a profit." He waves a hand. "You know how many people I've heard complain that their sex life was dead after being in a relationship for too long? That they didn't spend enough time with their significant others and they were desperate to connect? I realized it was an untapped market so I created Hush and fed the need. The new location takes the concept a step further."

"It's all a business decision, then. Not because you wanted to help people." Disappointment crashes through me, and I try to push it away. Of course. It's always a business decision. My brother thinks the same way. So does my father.

I sorta hoped Archer was different. Clearly, he's not.

"I'm not looking to help anyone. I'm no one's savior." His gaze meets mine and he tips his head toward me. "You of all people should know that."

I most definitely know that. "I find it funny that the man who is the epitome of anti-commitment creates a safe haven for couples looking to spice up their sex life." I shake my head. "You must see the irony."

"Oh, I do. Trust me." He smiles and the sight of that dimple I adore momentarily takes me aback.

"You should show Ivy some of the rooms," Gage suggests as he approaches us, breaking the quiet spell that had settled over Archer and me. I step away from him, smiling faintly at my brother, though really I'm irritated. I should be glad he spoke up before I did something foolish. Like touch Archer. Give away that I might . . . feel something for him.

I definitely feel nothing for him beyond a fondness for a man I've known for what feels like forever.

Ha. And a yearning for his body.

"I'd love to see the rooms," I say, trying to push the confusing thoughts from my brain.

"Yeah, Arch. Show her everything. Explain the concept behind the resort so she can get a better understanding." Gage smirks.

The look that crosses Archer's face is nothing short of uncomfortable. "Do you want to see them, Ivy?" he asks stiffly, his gaze flicking to Gage before it returns to me.

"Absolutely." I'm surprised he asks. I wonder more at his discomfort. Is this entire scenario misleading? Is he hiding some sort of secret sex den in one of the buildings? Oh, good lord, I know Archer's reputation precedes him, but he was pretty vanilla last night when we had sex. Nothing too outrageous.

But he was certainly the tastiest vanilla I've ever experienced.

We walk down a meandering gravel path, Archer leading us to a row of detached cottages that each individually house a room. They all have quaint front porches with a pair of large, comfortable-looking chairs on either side of the front entrance, and he approaches the largest one, me following right behind him and stopping while he opens the door.

Inhaling as discreetly as possible, I breathe in his scent, closing my eyes for the briefest moment. He smells . . . amazing, fresh and clean and delicious. I sway toward him, afraid I might fall into him, and he turns just as I right myself, his brows furrowed as he studies me.

"Ladies first." He points toward the door and I follow the length of his arm, realizing a little too late that the door is open and he's waiting for me to enter.

I'd been so caught up in my obsessive sniffing, I didn't realize he opened the damn door.

My cheeks hot, I walk inside, glancing about the space, which I instantly love. It's got a contemporary feel with dark wood floors, a giant fireplace dominating the room, and sleek furniture. I do a slow circle, taking everything in. I catch a glimpse of the giant bed within the bedroom, a deck off the back of the cottage with a beautiful view and—is that a . . .

"Is that a tub?" I point toward it lamely, feeling like a little kid.

"Yes, it is." He sounds amused, and he starts toward the French door that leads onto the deck. I follow him, curious to check it out, and I glance over my shoulder, seeing that Gage isn't following us.

In fact, he isn't in the room at all.

Frowning, I turn back around to see Archer studying me carefully, his hand curled around the door handle. "Your brother took a phone call. He's out front."

"Oh." Swallowing hard, I nod once. Is that all I can seem to say when he makes those types of statements? The ones that worry me and make me realize that I can pretend I don't want him but it's all a lie.

I still want him. More now that I've had him.

"Well, let's check out the view then," I say, hoping he doesn't notice my wavering voice.

Being alone with Archer, even for a few minutes, is going to test my very patience.

Archer

IVY'S LOOKING AT me like she wants to eat me up with a spoon and fuck me, I'm returning the feeling a millionfold. But Gage is out front and who knows how long he's going to take with his call.

I can't risk it.

I want to risk it so bad my hands literally itch to touch her.

Being near her flat out arouses me, there's no denying it. Her scent, her smile, the way she looked at me when I explained Hush's background. I saw the glimmer of sympathy in her eyes. She knows what an asshole my father is.

The last thing I want from her is sympathy. I'm not a charity case.

She walks out onto the private deck and I follow her, admiring the curve of her ass, the little gasp of pleasure she gives when she catches sight of the rolling hills covered with what looks like endless rows of vineyards.

"So beautiful," she murmurs, and I wholeheartedly agree. She's gorgeous.

"You like the view?" Because I sure as hell do. I take a step closer, noting how I tower over her. Her hair is mostly dry, the ends wavy, and I want to grab hold of her ponytail. Yank her head back and kiss her until the both of us are stupid with lust.

"It's stunning." She glances over her shoulder at me, the smile on her face slowly fading. "You're looking at me weird."

The sexy whisper of her voice doesn't quite go along with what she's saying. "How am I looking at you?"

"Like . . . like you want something from me." She turns to face me but backs up a few steps, until she's leaning against the deck railing. Her hazel eyes are wide, her cheeks flushed. A few wisps of hair have escaped her ponytail, brushing against her face. I move toward her, slow and easy, not wanting to startle her. Not wanting to ruin this.

"I want nothing from you that you don't want to give," I murmur, and I note the rapid beat of her pulse at the base of her throat.

"Archer." Her voice is a warning, with the slightest bit of waver. That waver gives me hope. "My brother is right out that front door. What if he finds us?"

"We're not doing anything that we need to hide." I'm directly in front of her, crowding her, and I rest my hands on the railing on either side of her body, effectively trapping her.

"Yet," she whispers, and that one single word gives me so much damn hope, I do what I've been dying to do since I saw her in the hallway of my house.

Dipping my head, I nuzzle her hair with my cheek, breathing in her scent, closing my eyes. My entire body tingles at having her close, hearing the catch of her breath, feeling the slight tremor that moves through her. She doesn't touch me, doesn't so much as move, and I settle my mouth close to her ear. "All I can think about is last night."

"Archer." She sounds like I'm torturing her.

Good. Feeling's mutual.

"Do you think about it? I swear to God, Ivy, all I want to do is drag you into that bedroom right now and fuck you until you can't see straight." My control is about to snap. And I never let it snap. But this woman pushes all my buttons, does everything she can to tear me apart with just a look. A smile. It blows my mind how much power she wields over me.

She has no clue about her power either.

"You shouldn't talk to me like that. Last night was a . . . mistake." She settles her hand on my chest as if she's going to push me away, but her fingers curl ever so slightly into my shirt. Pulling me just a fraction closer to her.

Triumph surges through me. She can't resist this pull between us either. "You really think so?"

"I know so." She pushes at my chest so I have no choice but to look at her. She's not strong enough to get me to step back, though. No way am I moving from her yet. "We can't continue this."

"You want to." It's a statement, not a question.

"No I don't." But she's nodding as I lean into her, and when I brush my mouth with hers, the shuddering exhale she breathes against my lips twists up my insides. "Archer . . ."

I love hearing her say my name, even if it's in protest. Because really she's not protesting. She wants this just as bad as I do.

"Just one kiss," I murmur against her lips, darting out my tongue to lick. The soft moan that escapes her is my answer, and I settle my mouth fully on hers, our tongues meeting, circling, tasting. I rest my hand on her hip, stepping into her, wanting to feel her.

The breeze sweeps over us, a shiver moves through her, and I slip my arms completely around her waist, tugging her lower body close to mine. Fuck Gage. Fuck anything else. I want to pull her into that bedroom, slam the door and keep her in the bed pinned beneath me for the next twenty-four hours.

It wouldn't be enough. But when it comes to Ivy, I'll take what I can get.

A buzzing sound rings through my head as I continue to kiss her, lose myself in her. I slide my hands over her ass, groaning when she grinds subtly against me. The buzz gets louder, more insistent, and I break the kiss first, staring down at her, my breath coming in pants. "What is that?"

She blinks up at me, looking as wrecked as I feel. "I think it's your phone."

Shit. She's right. I can feel it vibrating in my jeans pocket. Yanking it out, I see it's a text message from Gage.

I gotta get back home. Meet me at the car.

"It's your brother." Damn it, I'm not ready to send her back to the city with Gage. I want to keep her here with me.

Like she'd ever go for it. She has a life. A relatively new career, friends—she probably has little time to spare, especially for me.

I'm delusional if I think I can make something between us work. Not that I want something real or lasting. A fling. That's all I want. And then there's the bet to consider.

You're really going to let a bet guide your decision?

I ignore the shitty little voice in my head.

"What did he say?" She licks her lips as if she's trying to get one last taste of me, and my cock twitches as I reluctantly step away from her.

"He's ready to leave."

"That's probably best." She pushes away from the railing, glancing to her left, looking at the tub that sits outside near the deck. "You never did explain the reason for the tub being outside."

"It's built for two. The decks are all private; none of the guests can see each other." I smile, imagining the two of us in that tub, our naked skin slick and soapy, Ivy sitting in my lap, her long legs wound around my waist. "It's, uh, one of our most popular features."

"I'm sure." The sarcasm is thick and I take another step away from her, surprised. "Archer, what happened between us last night . . ."

"Was a mistake. I totally agree." I finish for her, needing to be the first one who said it.

Weird thing, though, is the look on her face when I did. Like I slapped her when she least expected it.

"A mistake," she says slowly as she nods. "That's what you think?"

"Absolutely. I mean, come on. We could never work. I don't do relationships. You know this." I sound far more confident than I feel. Maybe it's because I always say this sort of thing to women, or really more to myself. I've never been in a relationship. I know I would fail at one. I would most definitely disappoint her. Ivy.

But secretly? I wish she would give me—give us—a chance.

"And I do."

"You most definitely do," I agree a little too quickly.

"And you're yet another Humpty Dumpty." She sighs.

"What?" Okay, that made no damn sense. Why is she calling me Humpty Dumpty?

"The kind of guy who's all broken up and can't be put back together again." She smiles at me, but it's sad and the sight of it makes me feel like a complete jerk. "I have a type. And I think you top my type list."

"I'm on your type list?" I never believed Ivy had any sort of crush on me. Not beyond the *push-pull-we-hate-each-other-maybe-we-should-tear-each-other's-clothes-off* thing we've been suffering through for years. Though I always figured that was more one-sided on my part.

"I never realized it until now. You're so right. We could never work. I'm too nice. And you're too . . . you." She drops that bomb like it makes all the sense in the world.

"What's that supposed to mean?" I rub my palm against my chest, irritated with myself. I'm acting butt-hurt over a woman. This is crazy.

"Do I really need to explain myself, Archer?" She doesn't let me answer. "Let's go meet Gage. I need to get out of here."

Without a word, I follow her out, trying to ignore the disappointment settling over me like a heavy wet blanket.

But I can't. Her rejection, her words hurt far more than I care to admit. And I'm the one who rejected her first.

We're quiet as we head back to the car, Gage waiting beside it with his arms crossed in front of him, tapping his foot impatiently. We all get inside, Ivy taking the back seat this time, and the mood is dark as I make the quick drive home.

They both hop out of my car as if they can't wait to get

away from me the moment I pull up in front of my house and I climb out, chasing after them.

"Sorry to be so abrupt, bro," Gage tosses out apologetically as he yanks his keys out of his pocket and hits the remote, unlocking his car. "I have a client wanting to meet for dinner. He owns a piece of property I've been after for months and I think he's finally going to cave."

"I understand. You'll have to call me when you make the deal."

"Prepare for a call late tonight then." Gage grins at me and I chuckle.

I get it. I'm a businessman. When an opportunity presents itself, you have to go for it, and that's exactly what Gage is doing.

Sort of what I did with Ivy.

Sprinting ahead of her, I approach Gage's Maserati and open the passenger door for her, watching as she slides into the seat. She glances up, her eyes fathomless as she studies me. "Thank you, Archer," she murmurs. Then adds meaningfully, "For everything."

"You're welcome," I automatically say, though I'm not quite sure what we're referring to.

Rolling her eyes, she huffs out a breath and yanks the door closed, effectively shutting me off.

Shutting me out.

And as I watch the car speed away, I feel like I'm watching my heart leave with it, forever in Ivy's possession.

Fucking crazy, but true.

Chapter Eight

Ivy

One week later.

"AND SO YOU had sex with him."

I nod miserably, trying to ignore the glee in my friend Wendy's voice. She's really enjoying my story—a little too much. "I did."

"And it was awful. Terrible. He was selfish and didn't bother getting you off."

"Wendy," I whisper harshly, glancing about the restaurant, at the people sitting nearby. Nobody's paying us any mind. "What if someone heard you?"

"No one heard me. And quit trying to change the subject. Give me all the dirty details." Wendy sips from her water glass, her brows raised expectantly.

I sigh, completely put out and embarrassed that she

wants to hear everything, yet also perfectly willing to reveal all. I've had no one to talk to about my encounter with Archer and I've been holding this inside me for an entire week.

Then I see Wendy waiting for me at our usual restaurant for our Saturday lunch date, and I immediately tear up like a baby when she asked what's new.

I reached my breaking point.

She took one look at my tear-streaked face, my watery eyes, and demanded I tell her what the heck was wrong with me. After purging the entire story of my encounter with Archer in twenty minutes, she's contemplating me with a gleam in her eye, as if she sees me in a new light. She's probably impressed—or in shock. I don't normally do this sort of thing. Wendy's the adventurous one with men. I'm the boring one who tends to choose wrong and stay too long.

I definitely don't do one-night stands with sexy-as-hell men who know just how to touch me to make me go off like a rocket. No man has ever been able to make me go off like a rocket. Ever.

Until now. Until Archer.

"He wasn't selfish," I say primly, pressing my lips together to keep from saying what I really want to.

He's amazing. Hot as hell. The best kisser ever. Oh, and his hand . . .

A slow smile curves Wendy's mouth. "Meaning he was all right."

Better than all right. "He knew what he was doing."

"Quit being so vague." Wendy sounds irritated. Not that I can blame her. I'm being vague on purpose.

"I'm not about to give you any more detail than that. Sorry," I say chirpily, sipping from my water glass. "I don't kiss and tell."

"Since when? We've dished about plenty of men. Now I want details about the one who was actually decent in bed and you're not talking." Wendy's eyes narrow as she contemplates me. "What gives?"

I squirm in my seat. I don't want to admit that my night with Archer is ... special. She'll probably make fun of me. She *should* make fun of me. I deserve it. I'm thinking like an idiot. "I really don't want to relive what happened between Archer and me. It's too weird. We've known each other for too long."

I'd have hoped he would call but he hasn't. We agreed it was a mistake, what happened. I walked away from him. The subject was closed, in both my mind and his.

But I lied to myself. Since I came home from Napa, he constantly invades my thoughts. I'm trying my best to focus. I throw myself into my work, which is easy considering how busy we are. Sharon Paxton is one of the most coveted interior designers in the city and her clientele keep her—and me—busy. Learning from her, working with her is a privilege, one I take very seriously.

I've lost concentration more than once, though, since the Archer incident. I missed an appointment with a very important client. I brought the wrong fabric samples to another one. I was acting so out of character, Sharon sat me down yesterday afternoon and asked what was wrong. I made up some sort of excuse, promised I would do better and escaped her hawk-like gaze before she asked any more questions.

This is what Archer's done to me. Turned me into a terrible employee. I can't sleep. I sit around on the couch at night and watch really bad reality TV. All the while I stare at my cell phone, willing him to call me, text me, something.

Yes. I've turned into one of those girls. God help me.

Our waiter magically appears with our lunch, setting our salad orders in front of us before he takes off, leaving me alone once again with my too nosy, too perceptive friend.

"You like him," she says, stabbing her fork into her salad with relish. Like she's killing the lettuce.

"No way," I reply too quickly. I'm such a liar. "He drives me crazy. He always has."

"Because you like him. You just didn't realize it yet. Now you do. The two of you have sex and it's like roses and romance and you want more," Wendy says, full of logic.

The sex between us was definitely not roses and romance. I can't begin to describe what it was like, but not soft and sweet like I was used to. It was hard and fast and immensely satisfying. "No, it wasn't quite like that."

"But it was good."

"It was amazing," I admit softly, earning a giant smile from Wendy.

"Knew it." She munches happily on her salad while I sit and watch her, my appetite having fled a while ago. "Call him. Tell him you want to do it again."

"No way." I shake my head, jealous of Wendy's hearty appetite. I've hardly eaten since my night with Archer. He's all I can think about and it's so stupid, I don't know why I'm acting this way. "I don't want to do it again."

"Liar."

"Okay, your smug, short answers are starting to bug," I say, grabbing my fork and stabbing the lettuce much like I saw Wendy do a moment ago. Damn it, I'm going to eat even if it kills me. "And they're totally not helping my situation."

"Well, what are you going to do then? You and Archer Bancroft have a past. A history. There's tension there and it finally resulted in the two of you having hot, amazing, outrageous sex."

I don't answer. I'm not going to give her the satisfaction of an acknowledgement.

"Now you're all mopey and sad. Wishing you could see him. Well, go see him then. Call him up. Greet him with, 'Hey sexy, let's do *that* again.' See what he says." Wendy smiles. "I bet he'd take you up on your offer."

But what if he didn't. "I would never call him and say something like that."

"Maybe that's half your problem."

I glare at her and she bursts out laughing. "It's not funny," I insist.

"I think you like him more than you want to admit, and you don't know how to deal with it. I'm trying to tell you how to deal." Wendy offers me a sympathetic smile. "Maybe you need to fess up to your feelings. Why are you acting this way? Is it because you're disappointed in yourself for doing something so crazy?"

"Partly." I shrug. "I don't know why I'm acting like this. Why he has me all twisted up in knots."

"I've already told you why," Wendy says gently. "There's nothing wrong with you contacting him. I'm sure you're waiting for him to call because that's your usual MO. Well, guess what. Having a one-night stand with Archer broke your pattern. Calling him will continue to break that pattern. And there's nothing wrong with doing things a little different."

Sighing, I stare at my still-full plate. My appetite has completely evaporated. "I was about to tell him that maybe I wanted to see him again, and he called our one night together a mistake. He doesn't want me, not like that." I should confess I called it a mistake too, but I can't. I hate to admit how much it hurt, him saying that. It's one thing for me to think it, another thing entirely to know he feels the same way.

But do I really feel that way?

No.

"Ah, honey . . ."

I interrupt her. I really don't want any sympathy. There's no one to blame for this but me. "Yeah, I might've changed up my pattern, but look where it got me? Miserable. Angry at myself for making such a stupid, *stupid* decision. He's not the one for me. Not that I ever really thought he was." I shake my head. "I need to focus on my anger over this."

"Yeah, you do," Wendy agrees.

"Not sit around wishing he would call." Whoops, wish I hadn't admitted that part.

"Forget him. Screw this guy," Wendy said vehemently.

"I already did." I scrunch my lips together.

We stare at each other across the table for a few seconds before we both burst into laughter.

"You sure did," Wendy says after she gets herself under control, slowly shaking her head as the occasional giggle escapes her.

Yeah. I sure did. What a mistake.

The realization hits me like a swift kick in the ribs. Yet again, I did it. I went after a man who has no intentions to do right by me. Heck, I have no intention of doing right by him. To do so would be utter foolishness. The man is a mess. He's a complete and utter mess and I have no one to blame but myself for getting involved with him.

I almost want to laugh at my mental choice of words. Involved. As if what we shared contains any sort of involvement beyond the quick and dirty sexual kind.

Archer Bancroft is my ultimate failure. That Humpty Dumpty of a man can never, ever be put back together again. I won't even bother trying.

Archer

"HEY, WHAT'S UP? Haven't heard from you in a while."

"I've been busy." So damn busy I can hardly breathe. Not so busy that I haven't been thinking of a certain someone constantly. Hence my reason for calling her brother—I'm digging for information. "You make that deal you told me about?"

"I sure did. Purchased the property for an absolute song. Already have a buyer lined up, and my end of the deal isn't even closed yet." Gage chuckles, sounding pleased with himself. "It all came together way too easy."

"That sort of thing usually makes me nervous." Struggles and roadblocks actually make me feel better when it comes to business. And life. When it's too easy, there's always a catch.

Always.

"I've been working this guy for over a year. This was definitely not an easy deal. I finally got him to cave. I'm a persistent motherfucker when I need to be." Gage full blown laughs.

Wasn't that the truth? One of the many traits Gage and I share. "Congrats man."

"Thanks." He pauses. "There must be another reason you called. You're not one for chitchat."

I blow out a harsh breath, working up my nerve. "Listen, I need Ivy's work number," I say as nonchalantly as I can, leaning back in my chair so I can stare out the window.

"Why? Call her cell." Gage sounds distracted. "Or are you afraid she won't answer you."

Damn Gage for being too perceptive. "I need to talk to her about a business proposition." Not a lie. The new location is going into fast-forward mode and the interior designer I hired to transform Hush is unavailable. I need someone quick.

I need Ivy.

"Are you serious? She's just a junior associate, you know. I have no idea if she's up to snuff with what you might need." Gage mutters something under his breath, and I hear a female's soft laugh.

"Way to bag on your sister." I shake my head, irritated with him. "And where the hell are you anyway?"

"Work. Where the hell are you?"

Doesn't sound like he's at work. And he's awfully quick on the defense. "Come on, just give me her number."

"Hold on, I need to scroll through my contacts. Give me a minute."

Tapping my fingers impatiently against the edge of my desk, I wait. I can hear Gage say something, hear the light tones of a woman answering him, and I wonder who he's with on a Monday afternoon. Can't help but feel a little jealous too.

Jealousy is an emotion I'm not used to and definitely not comfortable with. There's no need to get jealous if I'm never with a woman beyond a night or two, right? I move through life with no entanglements, no relationships beyond my friendships, and even then I don't let many into my inner circle. Hell, I don't even stay in regular contact with my mom, not that she cares. She's too busy hitting the bottle or fighting with my father. And I deal with him only because I have to.

More than one woman has described me as a loner. Fairly accurate. I surround myself with plenty of people but it's meaningless. A good time for a few hours before I go home alone. Socially I've withdrawn as I become more consumed with work. This latest project has kept me constantly going these last few weeks.

I miss Ivy. I regret calling what happened between

us a mistake. It wasn't. Screw the bet, forget my friends, forget everything. I want to see her. It's been over three weeks. Three long weeks without seeing her pretty face, that gorgeous smile. Hell, I miss hearing her all exasperated with me, insulting me, telling me to leave her alone.

I miss the way her body felt beneath mine. How she tugged on my hair tight, the hot little words she panted against my lips just before I made her come.

"All right, here you go," Gage says, interrupting my thoughts as he rattles off a number. I scribble it across a notepad, my mind still foggy with images of Ivy, and I blink hard, banishing her as best I can. She is the last thing I need to think of while I'm talking to her brother.

"Thanks," I mutter, dropping the pen on my desk and scrubbing my hand over my face. I need to get a grip.

"You're serious about wanting to hire her?"

"I am. The new Hush location's completion is ahead of schedule and I'm pushing it forward. Our previous designer is heavily involved with another project, so she's unable to get on board. I thought I'd ask Ivy if she's available," I say this as casually as possible, not wanting him to figure out my other motive for contacting her.

"I know her boss would probably like a chance at it," Gage says.

Sharon Paxton probably would. But I know for a fact she's beyond busy with her own clients. She has a waiting list, for the love of God. This probably doesn't bode well with getting Ivy's help, but I'm willing to pay whatever it takes to have her work with me on this project.

I want to see her that badly. This is the perfect excuse. That I have to use my business as a way to get her back into my life is probably underhanded, but I don't care. I'm to the point that I'll do anything to see her again.

Prove to her that maybe I am worth being put back together again.

"I'm sure she would," I say. "I'd rather have Ivy."

Gage is quiet for a moment before he finally asks, "Do you have a thing for my sister?"

"Not at all," I say easily. "Hell, we argue most of the time when we see each other."

"Then why would you want to work with her if all you do is argue?"

Valid question. Shit. "I trust her. I've known her for years. She's your sister. She'll do a good job and not try and screw me over."

"Huh." Gage doesn't sound like he believes me so I push forward.

"This project, this location, it has to be handled delicately. Discreetly. I can't hire any designer off the street. I need someone I can trust to keep their mouth closed and not leak what I have planned."

"You haven't even told me what you have planned," Gage points out.

"Exactly, and I'm not going to either. That's why I think Ivy is the perfect fit." This part is true. I do want her to work for me. I trust that she won't blab what I have planned for the remote location. An even sexier, more intimate resort than Hush, it will cater to wealthy couples that want an indulgent getaway with their significant other.

Private gourmet meals, couples massages, the small hotel will be exclusive to only eight couples at any given time. The location will be the ultimate in intimate, quiet luxury.

"Well, good luck. Give her a call. I'm betting she'll say no."

"Why does everything circle back to a bet?" I ask irritably, not needing the reminder. "And how do you know she'll say no?"

But she doesn't count toward the bet, right? Didn't Gage and Matt count her out? After all, she's just Ivy.

"She doesn't particularly like you, Archer. You know this." Gage makes it sound like common knowledge. "And besides, I'm going to guess her boss won't let her take on the project. Sounds like it'll be over Ivy's head."

"I want her. Only her." I clear my throat, realizing how that sounds. "For the project," I add weakly.

"Good luck. I doubt you'll get her, but more power to you."

Gage's words are just the challenge I need to hear.

Chapter Nine

Ivy

"Chicken, I need your help."

Icy shock moves through my veins at the first sound of Archer's familiar, deep and sexy-as-hell voice. The very last person I expected to call me at my office on an early Wednesday afternoon—and just how did he get my work number anyway?

Duh, your brother.

Freaking Gage.

"No, 'Hello, Ivy, how's it going?' And I really, *really* wish you wouldn't call me chicken." I'm trying to joke. Or more like trying to figure out if he really does need my help. I mean, come on. Like hearing from him out of nowhere nearly a month later, after what happened between us, is no big deal.

It's *such* a big deal.

"So nice to hear from you, Archer. What's it been, a couple days?" Almost twenty-five days, not that I'm keeping count.

"Very fucking funny, Ivy. I'm not kidding," he growls irritably. "I need your help, and I needed it yesterday."

"And you're calling me? Why? How exactly can I help you?" Wow, I sound remarkably cool and calm, but deep within my insides are trembling. And for whatever crazy reason, my nipples are hard. All from his gruff, commanding tone. So ridiculous, but it's like the second I hear his voice, my body reacts. I haven't been able to get that night out of my mind. Images of a naked Archer above me, kissing me, buried deep inside me are burned on my brain.

"You're still single, right?" he asks, knocking me from my thoughts.

"How is that any of your business?" My heart lodges in my throat. As if he would care. "And who told you that?" Fine. I so am. I haven't talked to Marc, the jerk, since I broke it off with him. And I haven't talked to any other guy either, let alone gone out on a date since my night with Archer.

Has he somehow ruined me forever? God, I hope not. I'm only twenty-four. I don't want to die a shriveled up old lady pining for a man who had sex with me once and then walked away.

"Gage told me."

I'm going to kill my brother. "Why do you care if I'm single or not?"

"I have a proposition for you." He pauses and my

heart falls into my stomach with hope. "A business proposition."

Of course. Not that I expected a sexual one. Hello, been down that road once before and look where it got me? A lot of lonely, achy nights waking up after sweaty, too-graphic dreams involving me and him naked. "What sort of business proposition could you possibly have for me?"

"We're getting ready to open a new set of suites at Hush. There's only a handful, but they're bigger, much more exclusive—and expensive—and I need someone to design the interior." He pauses and my heart squeezes. "I want you."

Hearing his familiar, deep voice say he wants me in that commanding way of his sets my legs shaking. And I'm sitting down. Ridiculous. "Maybe I'm busy," I say haughtily, which is true.

"Come on, Ivy. You're not too busy for me, are you?" He's teasing me, but there's a sexual edge to his voice. One I want to ignore.

"Actually, I am. I have a lot of projects I'm working on currently for clients." I sound like a prim schoolteacher, but damn it, I know I have an appointment I need to get to soon. I really don't have time to listen to him go on and on about how much he *needs* me. Getting my hopes up only for them to come crashing down when he never contacts me again.

He's real good at that.

"I'll make it worth your while." His voice lowers, deceptively soft yet edged with smoky, sensual heat.

Tingles sweep over my skin. "I'm sure you will," I say sarcastically. I refuse to let him know how much he still affects me, especially after he so callously ignored me this past month.

We got naked together. We had sex. And he acts like it never happened. I do too, because how else should I handle it? Confront him?

Hey, what the hell was that night all about anyway? I felt the earth move and thought maybe . . . you felt the same?

Can't go there. No matter how badly I want to. And wasn't he the one who called it a mistake?

Yeah, so not going to bring any of that up to him. He'd rather forget. Just like I would.

Liar.

I wish he hadn't called. Just hearing his voice works me up. Archer Bancroft is dangerous for my well-being and I know it. Delicious. Wicked. Appealing. Wrong. At least, he's wrong for me.

"I have to go, Archer." I keep my tone brusque as my gaze lands on my computer screen. My to-do list mocks me, it's so long. And my calendar app dings, reminding me I have an appointment with a client in thirty minutes.

Which means I need to leave now if I want to make it on time.

"Listen, I'm in town and I want to see you," he says, shocking me. I didn't expect him to say that. "Let me take you to dinner tonight and I'll explain everything. How about we go to Spruce?" He refers to an ultrapopular restaurant not too far from my office. I've been there before and it's amazing. Amazingly intimate too—the perfect restaurant for a date. Not that we're going on a date.

Yeah, right.

"I'll pick you up at your office, we can have a few drinks first, then dinner," he continues.

"No," I say vehemently, rendering him completely silent. I'd bet a million dollars not many women utter that word in his presence, but the very last thing I want is Archer invading my private workspace, spreading his devastating charm all over it.

I really don't need that reminder lingering around long after he's gone. Some things should remain sacred from the Archer effect. "How about I meet you at the restaurant?"

He's silent for a moment. Like he doesn't approve of my suggestion. As if I care. "That should work," he finally says, his words clipped.

"Is seven too late?" I glance at my calendar, see that I have one last meeting with a new client at five-thirty to go over wallpaper samples, but the restaurant he suggested isn't too far from the office. I could probably make it on time.

"I'm staying the night in the city so seven's perfect." He pauses, the silence heavy with unrecognizable . . . tension. "It'll be good to see you again, Ivy."

Clutching the phone tight, I close my eyes for the briefest moment, all those unwanted memories bombarding me. The way he kissed me, the taste of his lips. How he'd touched me, his big hands everywhere, settling between my legs, teasing me while he murmured the hottest, sexiest words I'd ever heard.

And that was only the moment out on the terrace. Never mind later, when we ended up naked in a bed. I can't even go there. Not now, with his velvety deep voice in my ear.

"Seven o'clock at Spruce," I confirm, opening my eyes to glare unseeingly at the computer. "See you then."

I hang up before he can say another word, proud of myself. Women don't hang up on Archer either. Hell, no one really hangs up on him. He's a force to be reckoned with.

And now he calls me out of nowhere declaring he needs me—please. He's stringing me along, I'm sure. Why, I haven't a clue.

But when do my past experiences with Archer ever make sense?

Deciding my client can wait a few minutes, I bring up Google and type in Archer's name, waiting breathlessly as a list of recent articles pop up. Talk of Hush and how he made it such a huge success. One article written a week ago catches my interest, about the expansion of the Hush brand and how he's refurbishing a location in Calistoga.

Frowning, I click on the link, reading the few details they have about the new Calistoga spot. He never mentioned it during the phone call. Or when we were last together and we were actually at Hush. He'd been so proud showing me everything. You think he would've at least mentioned a new location.

So why didn't he tell us about it?

Weird.

I close out Google and gather my things, my mind awhirl with what I read. Was this the job he referred to, the one he so desperately needs me for? All logical thought flowing through my brain is telling me not to bother meeting him. Cancel via text with no explanation. He would totally deserve it.

Curiosity rules me though, it always has. There's no way I can pass this dinner up. Despite how difficult it will be, sitting across from him for hours in a dark, intimate restaurant, gazing adoringly at his beautiful face. Wondering yet again how stupid could I be, having sex with him. Nursing this renewed crush of old that can go absolutely, positively nowhere.

I'm pitiful.

Archer

I GLANCE AT my watch for what feels like the millionth time, wondering where the hell Ivy is. She's close to twenty minutes late, and I know for a fact she's ridiculously punctual.

With the exception of tonight when she's meeting me. Shit.

Drumming my fingers atop the white tablecloth in a steady rhythm, I glare at the entrance to the restaurant. I hate it when people make me wait. In business, I flat out don't tolerate it. That this woman I've known since she was a gangly teenager with a mouthful of metal leaves me waiting almost desperately for her arrival blows my mind.

And rarely is my mind blown. Funny, how the one person who keeps doing it on a regular basis is Ivy.

She's angry with me. I could hear it in her voice when I spoke to her on the phone. It had taken me two days to work up the courage to call her. Like a complete wuss, I rehearsed that conversation in my mind a thousand times.

The reality had turned out worse than my imagination. At least I got her to agree to see me. But what if she decides not to show and leaves me hanging?

I push the thought from my mind, refusing to acknowledge it for even a minute.

"Another drink, sir?" The waitress appears, her gaze full of sympathy. She probably thinks I've been stood up.

Hell, I've never been stood up in my life. "I'm fine," I mutter.

"Perhaps you'd like to order dinner? An appetizer, maybe?" She sounds hopeful and I'm beyond ready to crush her dreams.

Shaking my head, I glare at her. "I'll wait a few more minutes."

She takes off after flashing me a wan smile, leaving me to brood. If Ivy doesn't show, I can hire someone else to do this job. It wouldn't be a problem, there's a goddamn list of designers who would give up their first born to work with Bancroft.

But damn it, I trust her. I want her. And not just for her amazing design skills.

She isn't *just* Ivy. Could I really fall for her? Why else would I act like such an anxious asshole? This woman has me so twisted up in knots I'm ready to do anything to have her back in my life.

Anything.

Scowling, I glare at the door, as if that'll make her magically appear. I'm thinking like a chick but I can't deny it. I want her with me all the damn time. It's scary how bad I need her. Trying to ignore her didn't work. I went almost an entire month without contacting her, but she's all I could think about. The moment I get into the city, I'm reaching for the phone, demanding that she meet me.

I remember how put out she sounded on the phone, her voice full of irritation. The first indication I'm most likely going to screw this up.

Hell. I cannot screw it up.

And then there's the stupid bet. Matt sends me the occasional email asking on my dating situation. Hell, he haunts my Facebook page, probably just waiting for me to change my status from "single" to "in a relationship".

As if I ever would do that. I know his ass is watching. I won't give him the satisfaction.

The front door opens, letting in a gust of cold air that chills my skin, sends a rush of awareness through me that nearly steals my breath. *She* enters the dimly lit restaurant, windblown and gorgeous, her curvy body covered by a black coat. I greedily drink her in as Ivy pushes wild strands of long dark brown hair away from her face, her gaze searching the room before those pretty hazel eyes light upon me.

I work to keep my expression neutral, my mouth curving into a subtle closed-lip smile, but inside I burn.

For her.

She smiles in return, though it's faint, and the sight of it is like a punch to the solar plexus. I wait impatiently as the hostess takes Ivy's coat before leading her to my table.

The way Ivy moves captivates me. Sinful and sexy yet with an innocent air, her hips sway as she heads toward me, the skirt of her black dress swishing about her legs. The dress covers her completely, but I know exactly what it's hiding beneath the clingy fabric. All I can think about is slipping my hands beneath her skirt so I can touch her thighs. I remember the first time I touched them, how they trembled. How smooth her skin was . . .

"Sorry I'm late," she says as she sits quickly, not giving me time to stand and greet her like I want to, with a hug. I wanted another chance to get my hands on her again, however briefly.

Ivy smiles up at the hostess as she pushes the chair in for her before hurrying away. "My meeting took much longer than I anticipated," she explains apologetically. Always polite, though I see the strain around her mouth, in her entire expression. She's uncomfortable being with me. I get it.

I don't like it, but I get it.

"Trying to keep me on my toes?" I raise my brows and she frowns.

"I didn't do it on purpose, Archer." She exhales shakily. "I'm not interested in playing games with you."

"I don't want to play games with you either, Ivy," I say. God, I wish I could reach out and touch her. Rest my hand on hers. Tell her how much I miss her.

She sounds breathless, which makes my body twitch. Reminding me how breathless she'd been the last time I saw her—naked. How she begged for more when I had her pinned beneath me, her body shaking as I made her come with my name falling from her lips.

Having her sitting in front of me after not seeing her for a month is like a shock to my system, leaving me tongue-tied. Frozen. She picks up the menu, oblivious to my dazed stupor, and smiles when the waitress approaches, ordering a glass of wine.

"Want another beer, sir?" The server's cheerfulness grates.

"Yeah," I bite out, scowling at the waitress just before she hurries away. I catch Ivy sending me a secret smile as she shakes her head. Makes me wonder if she thinks I'm some sort of joke or something. The way she looks at me, like I amuse her.

Better than sending me the cold glare of death, which I suppose I deserve after how I've treated her since we were together.

"You look good," I say, my rough voice startling her from her quiet perusal of the menu.

She flicks her gaze up, those pretty eyes meeting mine. "It's . . . nice to see you too, Archer." Her voice is the stuff of my wet dreams, low and melodic. "Have you already ordered?"

"I was waiting for you." Damn, does she think I'm a total rude bastard or what?

Most likely—you are, after all.

"Oh. Well isn't that sweet of you." She checks out the

menu again, biting her lip as she looks over her options. The restaurant's packed, the buzz of conversation a low hum that falls away the longer I watch her.

What would it take to get back into her good graces? What do I have to prove?

Everything.

The waitress reappears, snapping me from my thoughts, and I order the steak while Ivy orders seared scallops. The server takes our menus, promises our drinks will be ready in minutes and then leaves us alone.

Finally.

Ivy watches me expectantly as she takes a sip of water, the delicate gold bracelets on her arm jingling with the movement. "So tell me about this job and why you need me so badly," she says, getting right to the point.

I toy with my empty beer bottle, unsure how to start what will surely be an awkward conversation. It's going to take everything I have not to blurt out why I really want her to work for me. "I'm opening a new location."

A little smile teases the corners of her lips. "I saw."

"Where? Ah, let me guess. Online." Her gaze meets mine and I stare at her, probably looking like a lovesick fool. She nods in answer, her gaze cutting away from mine, and I feel oddly defeated. "It's in Calistoga. I've been in negotiations on the property for a while and at one point it almost fell through. But I finally put the deal together and we've been doing a quick renovation on it the last few months."

"So you knew about this when you—when you showed Hush to Gage and me?" Her smile disappears when I nod. "Why didn't you tell us about it?" She sounds shocked.

"I've been keeping it a secret. I didn't want anyone to know. Most details about the location are pretty limited and I made sure of that. I don't want anyone to know what we're offering to our guests until we open." I shrug.

"So now the new resort is almost ready?" She's studying me like I'm crazy, which I probably am.

"Two months, give or take." I shrug.

"So why are you here when you should be back in Calistoga supervising the remodel?"

Here comes the tough part. The stuff I don't want to admit for fear she'll laugh in my face. "I wanted to meet with you," I say, my voice stiff.

"You came here for the sole purpose of seeing me?" She sounds incredulous, visibly swallowing as she reaches for her water glass, her shaking hand making the ice rattle against the glass when she sets it down. She looks nervous.

Welcome to the club. I'm nervous. And women don't make me nervous.

With the exception of Ivy.

"This project is important. I want you by my side, Ivy, working with me."

"I—I don't understand where this is coming from. You've never come to Paxton before. You haven't even seen my portfolio."

"I saw samples of your work online." Everything's online, both a wonderful and scary thing. "Your portfolio is on the Paxton website."

"Oh," she says weakly, settling back in her chair, her

shoulders sagging, her lips parted as if she wants to say something but can't come up with the words. She looks like she's in a state of shock. "Wha—what did you think?"

"Of your work? It's amazing." Giving into impulse, I reach across the table and grasp hold of her hand, giving it a gentle squeeze. "I know we'll be the perfect fit, that you'll be the perfect fit for Crave. Your sophisticated touch is just what the suites need."

"I—I don't know, Archer. What you're proposing is coming so out of left field, I don't know how to answer. I don't know if I can answer." She presses her lips together and shakes her head. "I have to talk to Sharon and see what she says, but I can already guess."

"What do you think she'll say?" It won't matter. I want Ivy on this project and I will pay and do whatever it takes to make that happen.

"She won't let me work on the project. She'll want it." Exactly what Gage pointed out, not that I'm surprised. In fact, I'm fully prepared, having already called Sharon and proposed my suggestion.

I'm not quite ready to admit the outcome of that conversation.

The waitress magically appears, interrupting what I might've said next by setting our drinks in front of us and I release my grip on Ivy's hand. We both thank her, our smiles polite and false. I see the way Ivy sneaks glances at me. Like she thinks I might've lost my mind.

I probably have.

The tension that has been brewing between us returns tenfold the moment the server makes her escape.

If I wasn't so damn agitated I might find it amusing, how Ivy took such a big gulp of wine, nearly draining her glass before she leans across the table. "You just can't come out of nowhere and demand I work for you, Archer," she whispers. "I answer to someone else. I just can't up and do what you want me to at the snap of your fingers."

"I already have approval from your boss."

Her eyes widen in shock. "What?"

I nod slowly. "I spoke with Sharon earlier. Explained my situation, how much I appreciate and am inspired by your talent, and knowing how busy she is, I would love to hire Paxton Design to work on this project for me. With the sole purpose of having you lead it."

She sucks in a harsh breath. "So I'm working for you."

"She cleared your schedule for the next two weeks. It'll be an intense, rushed job, but I know you can do it." I do. She's smart. Her employer had nothing but wonderful things to say about her, not that I'm surprised. Ivy is amazing.

So amazing, I can't stop thinking about her.

"What if I don't want to be a part of this project? What if I don't want to work directly with you?"

Damn, not the answer I expected from her. "Does it bother you?" Pausing, I study her, drinking in all that dark hair waving past her shoulders, her beautiful but shrewd gaze, her lips pressed together as if she's afraid she's going to say something she'll probably regret. "We've already done this, Ivy, and we were pretty damn compatible. Would it be such a hardship, having to spend time with me?"

Her jaw drops open, and she glances around as if she wants to make sure no one's listening before she leans across the table. "If you're implying that I'm going to have *sex* with you, you couldn't be further from the truth. Been there, done that, don't want to go through with it again."

"Ouch." I rub my chest, surprised by her words. Why, I'm not sure. I asked for them for saying all that. "Harsh."

"It's the truth," she retorts, draining the last of the wine in her glass. "God, I need a refill."

"I've made some mistakes. A lot of mistakes," I correct myself when she narrows her eyes, looking ready to blast me. "The biggest one is how I've treated you. I'm sorry I haven't called or contacted you since we were last together. I've been—busy." And too chickenshit to make the first move.

She rolls her eyes. "Like I was sitting beside the phone waiting for your call. Please, Archer. Don't flatter yourself."

She's extra feisty tonight, which I assume means she's extra mad at me. I need to tread lightly. "It's not that I was purposely ignoring you, you know. I've been swamped trying to put this new resort together." It's the best excuse I have—and the truth, for the most part. Hopefully she believes me.

Thankfully she doesn't acknowledge what I said. "Explain the new location. I'd love to hear more about your little secret," she says, settling back into her chair as if she's going to stay awhile.

Excitement rises within me. Her wanting to hear about it means she's interested. And once I get her fully hooked, she'll be on board to happily work with me. I know it. "It's the ultimate in luxurious comfort. Every need will be taken care of at the Calistoga location. It's a more intimate resort that caters exclusively to only a handful of couples at any given time. Couples that are looking to put intimacy back into their relationship. Even sexual intimacy." I stress the last two words.

"A swingers club," she states flatly.

I shake my head, chuckling. "Hell, no. What sort of pervert do you think I am?"

Ivy doesn't say a word, just arches a delicate brow in challenge.

I sigh and shake my head. "Fine, I'm a pervert. But I don't run a swingers resort, Ivy. There's no swapping with others or wild orgies going on at either location. It's all about a one-on-one level." Ironic, considering I have no clue what that's like.

"Then what exactly is this new place supposed to be?"

"It's whatever your heart desires," I say softly. "Whatever your lover wants. Hence the name Crave, considering it fits so perfectly. A discreet, comfortable safe place where you can discover your secret fantasies, indulge in your secret wants. The new location will provide whatever you might need, no questions asked."

Her cheeks are pink, her eyes wide. She looks almost . . . aroused. "It sounds—interesting."

I smile. Damn, she's beautiful. "It is. Very interesting."

She remains silent, tracing the stem of her wineglass with the tip of her index finger. I fixate on that finger, how delicately she touches the glass, the short, darkly painted nail. My skin suddenly feels too tight, I'm getting hard from watching her finger for the love of God. Taking a deep breath, I try to regain some control.

But hell, I'm dying to feel those fingers all over my body again . . . .

Leaning across the table, I lower my voice, ready to cut to the chase. "I need you, Ivy. I want you to bring a sexy, sophisticated touch to my resort."

A little sigh escapes her. "You've already arranged it with Sharon. Why feel the need to ask me?" She sips from her wine, her gaze steady on me over the rim of her glass.

"Because I want you to willingly work with me. I know I should've told you first before I spoke to Sharon, but I was getting desperate. I'm running out of time and I need to get this project finished. And I trust you." It's the truth. I hardly trust anyone. I definitely don't trust any women. They're all the same.

Except for Ivy.

Reaching for her hand again, I press my palm against hers and entwine our fingers. Hers are slender, delicate, and I swear they tremble in my grip. A jolt moves through me at the connection, as if my body missed being touched by hers. "Say yes, you want to work with me."

"It's not that easy . . ."

"Say yes," I repeat, refusing to take no for an answer.

"I shouldn't. I should be mad that you went above my head and made it happen anyway, with or without my approval."

I smile, feeling cocky. "Come on, you've never been able to resist me."

She tries to extract her fingers from mine but I squeeze tight, not about to let her go. "You're such an ass."

"You think I wouldn't use that to my advantage?" I

lower my voice. She's going to kill me for saying this, but I'm overcome. Having her hand in mine, our fingers laced together. I'm gripping her so tight, I feel like a desperate man. I haven't forgotten her no matter how hard I try. "I absolutely cannot get the last time we were together out of my mind."

"Please. We haven't spoken since. Until today." She glares at me with narrowed eyes, tugging against my hold, but I refuse to release her. "You know, I really can't stand you. Seeing you tonight only reiterates my feelings."

I don't doubt it for a minute. Most women hate me once they get to know me.

Not Ivy. She knows all my faults yet she still wants to be with me. Or at least she used to. I want that again. The closeness, that connection I share with no one else. She somehow understands me, she always has.

I know for a fact that not many people do.

"Fine, hate me all you want. Just say you'll do this."

"It's not that easy for me to walk away from my life, you know. I have responsibilities. And what if Sharon's mad that you did this?" I smooth my thumb across the top of her hand, and she releases a shuddering breath. "I'm asking for trouble, working with you."

"Ivy, please."

Her eyes widen at my choice of words. I rarely say please. I just take what I want. But please is not working with Ivy at this very moment. She looks ready to run.

"Archer . . ."

"Please, Ivy," I say again. "I need you."

Chapter Ten

Ivy

"It's HARD FOR me to believe you're serious." He's driving me crazy with how he's touching me. I can't think. And the way he's looking at me isn't much better.

At this very moment his sole focus is on me. That penetrating dark gaze of his locked on my face. As if nothing and no one else matters. All that intensity is tough to deal with.

Of course, he wants something from me. Not like he can be a complete ass and expect me to be agreeable.

Despite my instinct to scream *No!* and flee the restaurant, I take this moment to study him, my gaze roving over him greedily. He's wearing a black sweater that stretches across his chest, emphasizing his broad shoulders. His dark hair gleams beneath the soft glow of the lights shining from above.

More than one woman has glanced in his direction

since I sat down. Power, wealth, authority, it radiates from Archer in palpable waves. Funny how I can forget that when I'm not around him. How potent he is to my well-being.

Couple all that potency with a devastatingly handsome face and outrageously sexy body, no woman is immune.

Including myself, as much as I'm loath to admit it.

"What's so difficult for you to believe? I've already gotten your boss's approval. We're ready to move forward." He smiles, drags his thumb across my knuckles yet again. A bolt of heat rushes through me at the seemingly innocent touch. He knows what he's doing to me, how he affects me. This is an act to make me agreeable.

Stupid idiot that I am, I'm falling for it despite the warning bells screaming inside my head. "For how long again?"

"Two weeks tops."

How simple he makes it sound. He snaps his fingers and makes it all happen, just like that. Could I really stand to be around him for any extended length of time? I have no willpower when it comes to Archer. He's a weakness of mine. Like indulging in too much chocolate and bad movies on a Sunday afternoon.

Only a million times worse.

"And Sharon readily agreed to this without protest?" I found it hard to believe. She needs me around, she's so busy. I don't know how she can afford to let me go, even if it's only for two weeks.

"The prestige of her design company working with

Hush and Bancroft is more than enough incentive for her to have you come work for me." He pauses, the confident expression on his face downright breathtaking. "You really think she'd refuse me?"

Could anyone refuse him? He's a Bancroft, after all. And so arrogant with it, I wish I could tell him no. Just once. Right now would be the perfect time—but the opportunity he's offering me is just too tempting and Sharon would kill me if she's already agreed. He knows it too. "What you're suggesting . . . it's crazy. You really think we can get this project off the ground and ready in two weeks?"

"We can do whatever we set our minds to. Just say yes, Ivy." His gaze drops, landing on my mouth, where it lingers a fraction too long. My lips literally tingle, as if he physically touched them.

Extracting my hand from his grasp, relief floods me as I finally break the physical connection between us. When he touches me, I can't think. I have a problem thinking when he's looking at me too, so I drop my gaze. Study the tablecloth in front of me, which is a stark, pure white, made of fine, thick linen.

That I'd rather contemplate a tablecloth shows how powerful Archer's influence is on me. God, I'm weak when it comes to this man.

His sinfully deep voice breaks through my thoughts. "Stop playing this game, Ivy. It's going to happen."

Sighing, I reluctantly lift my gaze. "Fine. When do we leave?"

"Tonight?" He flashes that dazzling smile, the one that dissolves my panties. *Sexy, no-good jerk.*

Grabbing my wineglass, I drain it, my skin instantly warming from the alcohol. I'll definitely need more wine to get through the rest of this evening. "No way. Tomorrow."

"All right. Tomorrow works," he drawls. "But it'll have to be first thing. I have a few stipulations too."

"I'm sure you do."

"I'll need you to consult with me on everything. Every choice, every decision you need to make. It's not that I don't trust you, but there's a certain aesthetic I want at both locations and I need to ensure your choices meet that aesthetic."

I nod once. Nothing unusual there. "I don't have a problem with that."

"And if I don't like what you suggest, you won't try to convince me otherwise. I have final word." He wraps his fingers around his beer bottle and brings it to his mouth, taking a drink, gorgeously sexy when he swallows, which is insane.

He makes me insane. His scent, the way he watches me with that calculated, hot gaze. His mere presence warms my skin, sets fire to my blood. Floods me with memories of our one amazing night together. I both cherish and hate those memories.

And he's drawing out the suspense on purpose. I'm literally sitting on the edge of my seat, waiting to hear what he might say next. "I also want you to move in with me," he finishes once he sets the bottle down.

My mouth drops open, shock rushing through my veins. "Move in with you?" I squeak, clearing my throat.

"I'll need you on site every single day. I'm rushing this project. All decisions we need to make must be quick. I can't have you coming back and forth from San Francisco. I need you with me. Every day. Every night, until the project is finished. At the very least you can stay at Hush."

"Oh, I get exactly what you want from me." A slow-burning rage sweeps over me, making me shake. I push back my chair and stand, glaring down at him. "I'm not going to be another one of your sexual conquests."

Tilting his head back, he watches me, calm as ever. "Don't be angry, Ivy. I'm not asking you to have sex with me in order for you to have this project. I'm not that much of an asshole."

God, his words sting. What sort of woman does he think I am? "Yeah, right. Next thing I know I'm flat on my back in your bed. No thank you. You're not going to bribe me with career recognition either." Bending, I grab my purse from the floor and sling it over my shoulder.

"I know the idea of staying with me doesn't make you comfortable, but it's best for the project considering the timeline. Besides, I'm not asking you to wait for me naked in my bed every night, though the idea is appealing." The arrogance dripping from his voice makes me want to hit something. Preferably him. "Come on, I know you haven't forgotten how easy it was between us that night, Ivy," he murmurs, his voice low. Sexy.

Ugh.

His words enflame me, filling me with both lust and anger. I really hate that I still want him. "You're a bastard," I say through clenched teeth before I turn and head toward the door, desperate to escape the suddenly too warm, too confining restaurant.

I hear him call my name. Hear his chair scrape across the floor as he stands and starts to come after me. But I refuse to look back. Choose to ignore the hostess who's calling after me that she still has my coat.

Pushing open the door, I step out into the dark night, deeply breathing the cool air. A flash goes off in my face, I swear I hear them call Archer's name, and I head in the opposite direction, avoiding the paparazzi at all costs. How could I forget they follow Archer everywhere?

God. My head is spinning, and not just from the wine. The stupid photographer is just the tip of my overwhelming iceberg—that Archer demands I work for him. Going above my head to ensure I have no choice but to work for him is infuriating. Never mind that we had sex and he has to bring it up. Like he's trying to use that night against me. I could blame it on the champagne I drank too much of, I suppose.

So freaking embarrassing.

Worse? I know I would've done it without the champagne. I can't blame too much alcohol on my one night with Archer. I was completely sober.

But he's an asshole. A controlling, arrogant jerk who thinks I'm some sort of spineless, stupid girl. I wish I could refuse him but he's effectively trapped me. And why didn't Sharon talk to me about this? I can't quite wrap my head around how he made all of this happen and so quickly.

He's just that powerful, that influential to gain the things—or people—he wants with a simple phone call or snap of his fingers.

Not knowing which way to go, I turn right, heading blindly into the night. Cars pass by, I hear the loud rumble of a city bus as it speeds down the street, and I blink hard, my strides quick, my heart pumping like crazy. A shiver moves through me and I rub my arms with my hands, wishing I had my coat. It's a total favorite; I love that jacket and I'm pissed I left it in the restaurant like an idiot.

God, he's so distracting, it's unfair. Why did he have to be so gorgeous? So freaking irresistible?

I increase my pace, furious at my thoughts. I can hear him right now, following behind me, his determined steps hitting the sidewalk, his huffs of aggravation.

Good. I'm irritating him. Glad to know the feeling is mutual. I need to get away from him.

Far, far away.

"Ivy." The man is as tall as a god with legs as long as my entire body, meaning he easily catches up with me. His strong fingers clamp around my upper arm and he turns me so I face him. "Don't run away from me."

His words are spoken as a demand. "Let me go." I struggle against his hold and he tightens his fingers, making it impossible to escape.

Archer pulls me in close, his body heat wrapping around me, his potent scent filling my head, making me weak. "Stop fighting this."

I need my willpower to kick in. It has to or I'll never

survive him. "There's no 'this' to fight. I'm not help-ing you."

Archer looks downright offended at my words. "You don't have a choice. I need you."

"You don't need me. I'm just an easy target." The urge to punch him comes over me, stronger than ever. He has the advantage, knowing how easily I react to him. He's not above using it against me fully either. "I hate that you've done this," I murmur.

"Why?" His voice is deceptively soft. As persuasive as his fingers stroking my lower back, he's trying to lull me into a false sense of security. Like I'm some sort of cat he can pet and stroke and ease under his spell. I was strong enough before to send him away, to walk away on my own. But am I strong enough now? Can I resist him again? I don't know.

"You've already fooled me once." Not really, but it sounds good. We fooled each other. "I shouldn't let it happen again."

Reaching out, I rest my hand on his chest, desper-ate to push him away. It's as if my fingers have a mind of their own, though. I curl them into the soft, smooth fabric of his sweater, feeling the steely strength of him just beneath. A trembling sigh leaves me, and I keep my gaze locked on my hand, afraid to look at him. Afraid he'll see everything I feel for him reflected in my eyes.

"I was fooling myself," he finally says as he touches my cheek, slipping his fingers beneath my chin to tilt my head up. "I didn't mean to hurt you."

I frown. Did I hear him right? Did Archer just admit he'd done something wrong? "Well, you did."

Our gazes hold for long, quiet moments heavy with tension. I want to run. Break free of him once and for all and pretend this night never happened. Yet another part of me wants to stay. Wants to agree to what he's asking me. Maybe then I can get one of two things.

Either I can convince Archer we're truly meant to be. Or finally get him out of my system once and for all.

Archer

IVY'S FINGERS STILL grip my sweater, her innocent touch driving me fucking wild with wanting her. Holding her close, she fits against me perfectly, as if she were made for me. It was like this between us last time. The moment I pulled her into my arms, it was like we were two pieces of a puzzle that finally clicked together.

Half the reason I'd been scared shitless before. Still. No other woman feels this . . . right in my arms. And I haven't even kissed her yet. It feels damn good just to hold her, which is ridiculous because I don't need to just hold a woman.

I should have her sprawled naked and needy beneath me, screwing her brains out at this very moment. Forget emotion, forget everything but that driving need to consume. That's how I usually operate.

Yet here I am. Acting like I'm in junior high and holding hands with a girl for the first time. Terrified and out of my mind with it.

"Is this just an excuse to get in my pants?" she finally asks, her voice wary. She's so damn smart. "You wanting me to work for you in such close circumstances? Seems pretty desperate if you ask me."

Slowly shaking my head, I let my thumb drift across her plump lower lip. Only a month since I last kissed her and I can vividly remember her taste. The sounds she makes. The way she wound her arms around my neck, her slender fingers threading through my hair. Her touch had felt so damn good. Too good.

Fuck. That's exactly it. She's too damn good for me. I need to remember this.

"You're the only woman I can trust, Ivy," I murmur, my heart lodging in my throat, making it hard to speak. "The only woman who understands me and my life and my career and what's required. I know you won't leak any information about the new location. And I know I can trust you to help me make the right decisions when it comes to designing the interiors."

A trembling breath escapes her, the gust of air brushing against my thumb. My heart rate kicks up into a steady gallop and I inhale deeply. Trying my damnedest to act like she doesn't affect me.

But holy shit, does she ever affect me.

"How can I understand you when I don't even really know you, Archer? We've never been close." Her gaze drops to my lips, lingering there. "Despite what . . . happened between us last time, there's nothing between us."

I feel like there's too much between us, but I won't go there now. "You've been a part of my life for a long time. You've known me since I was a teenager. Before I became . . . this." The consummate playboy who can have any woman I want at any time. The workaholic hotelier who throws himself into his business until all he can do is live and breathe Hush. And now there's Crave . . .

"Yeah, well my feelings still haven't changed about you. I think you're crazy." She gasps when I lean in and brush my lips against the right corner of her mouth. That quick sample of her soft skin makes me ache for more. "Wh—why are you kissing me?"

"Because I need to." I kiss the left corner, moving to capture her upper lip between both of mine, nibbling a little bit before I release her. "I need your help, Ivy. I can't get the resort ready without you."

"Stop it." She's pushing at my chest but I'm not going anywhere. "Don't say things you don't mean."

"You really think I don't mean it when I say I need you?" I'm incredulous. I sure as hell need her. More than I care to admit.

I have to convince her back into my bed. At least one more time—possibly a few dozen times before I let her go back to her world and I go back to mine. She was there the night of Jeff and Cecily's wedding reception. All that pent-up chemistry swirling between us, exploding the moment my lips first touched hers. She knows how combustible it can be between us.

So why is she full of so much doubt?

"You don't need me. You just want me to bail you out of trouble. I've never mattered to you. Not really." She tilts her head away from mine when I lean in for another kiss.

"Damn it, Ivy," I start, but she cuts me off.

"You abandoned me, Archer." Ivy's voice is so soft, I can hardly hear her. "I know we agreed our having sex was a mistake, but the way you touched me in the suite at Hush right before Gage texted you, I was so confused. I thought you wanted . . . oh my God, I don't know what you want. Not really. I don't get you. Since I left you that afternoon, you haven't called. I haven't heard one peep out of you, not that I expected to." She takes a step back, withdrawing from me completely, and my arms feel empty without her in them. "This back and forth between us is . . . difficult. I can't risk getting close to you again only for us to end it before we really gave ourselves a chance. Not that there's an "us" . . ." Her voice trails off and her cheeks turn pink. She probably didn't mean to admit such a thing.

Her small admission gives me hope.

"I won't touch you. Unless you want me to." I smile but she doesn't return the gesture. Heaving a big sigh, I cup her cheek, briefly sliding my fingers across her soft skin before I let my hand drop away from her. I can't help but touch her, but if she doesn't want me to, I won't. "I promise."

Pressing her lips together, her hazel eyes go wide as she trembles. I draw her back into my arms, protecting her from the cold. She has to be freezing since she left her coat in the restaurant. "Let's get out of here and you can come back to the hotel with me downtown. I have the penthouse suite and the view of the city is amazing. It's too damn cold out here to talk."

Ivy stiffens in my arms just before she withdraws from me yet again. "Come with you back to your hotel room? I don't think so. Next thing I know, I'm flat on my back and you're all over me."

I smile. Damn, that sounds amazing. "And that's a bad thing, why?"

"Stop, Archer. I already told you I refuse to let that happen again." She crosses her arms in front of her, contemplating me with her shrewd gaze. "Besides, if we ever did have sex again, you'd run like you always do."

When shit gets serious, I definitely run. But not anymore. For once, I don't want to bail. "I can't run any longer, Ivy. This is it. I need the new resort to open with a roaring success. I need those suites to look amazing. Together, I know we can do it."

"Fine." She sighs. "We need to come up with a budget. A timeline." She taps her finger against her pursed lips, driving me wild with wanting her. Damn, she's beautiful. Even shivering in the cold, angry with me and most likely thinking I've lost my damn mind, she's gorgeous. Fucking amazing, really.

I don't deserve her help. I don't deserve Ivy Emerson whatsoever.

But I still want her. Desperately.

"We can plot and plan back at the hotel, Ivy," I tell her. "Come on. I won't try any funny business."

A perfectly manicured brow lifts at that remark. "Promise?"

Nodding, I make an X on my chest with my index finger. "Cross my heart."

"You swear? I can't think when you push yourself on me, Archer. And if you want my help in figuring out how we're going to do this, then you need me to be able to think."

Is it wrong that I'm pleased with her remark? That she can't think when I'm around? I love that, especially because I feel the same way.

"Come back to the suite with me, Ivy. We'll figure this out."

"Fine." She offers a jerky nod. "Let's do this."

Sweeter words were never spoken.

Chapter Eleven

Ivy

THE PENTHOUSE SUITE is amazing, not that I expect anything less. It encompasses nearly the entire top floor of the hotel, is larger than my apartment, and has three bedrooms, which reassures me. There will be no sleeping in Archer's bed tonight.

No matter how much I'm tempted.

I've stayed in more than a few Bancroft Hotels over the years, considering the Bancroft family comped my family all our rooms when we travelled, and I've never been disappointed. But I've never had any reason to stay at the Bancroft in downtown San Francisco. It's my hometown, after all.

"You like it?" Archer shuts the door and strides toward me, his voice full of pride. Despite the burden the family business has put on him his entire life, and specifically today, I know he's still proud of Bancroft, as he should be.

"The view is amazing." I approach the windows, staring out at the glittering view of the city before me. The moon breaks over the fog, shining its silvery light on the bay, and I withhold the sigh of longing that's desperate to escape me.

The beautiful suite, this gorgeous night ... is made for lovers. I yearn for that to be true, no matter how bad I know Archer is for me.

But Archer knows he needs to keep his distance. It's the only way I can stay sane.

God, how stupid could I be, pushing him away when I want him more than anything?

"I stay here whenever I come to the city. Better than staying at my parents', that's for sure." The bitterness in his voice is no surprise. He doesn't get along with his parents; he never has. Not that I blame him. His father treats him terribly. Their fractured relationship has always broken my heart.

He comes up behind me. I catch his reflection in the window and I hold my breath, marveling at how we look together. He towers over me, his dark hair mussed, his expression strained. As if he's as tense as I feel.

I can imagine his big hand sliding down my back, pushing gently so I have no choice but to bend forward. Hearing his dark, sexy voice commanding me to brace my hands on the shockingly cool glass. His skilled fingers would settle on my hips, slowly gathering the fabric of my dress so he could touch my bare skin beneath. Those assured fingers would slip beneath my thin panties to find me already soaking wet for him . . .

Lust surges through me and I stiffen my shoulders. God, I'm a wreck. He stands too close and I'm imagining how he'll take me right here, in front of a window for everyone to see.

"There is no 'us' in this room tonight, Archer," I say, my voice firm. No matter how much I want it to be true, I have to hold strong. The man is dangerous to my well-being. I want to smack myself for even contemplating going along with his stupid plan. I am so weak when it comes to him, it's pitiful.

"Well, that's unfortunate," he drawls, and I want to punch him.

God, I'm starving, and that's what's making me extra irritable. We left the restaurant before our dinners arrived, though Archer said he'd paid for them when he came out of Spruce. He called in room service from the car moments before we arrived at the hotel, ordering an enormous amount of food I would normally never eat. An assortment of appetizers, fried this and that, and I swear he even mentioned a pizza.

My stomach growls at the thought of pizza.

"Hungry?" He raises an eyebrow and I look away from him, embarrassed. Not that I'd ever admit to him I'm actually starved. Women don't eat, not in front of perfect men like Archer. We might nibble on a leaf of lettuce and drink copious amounts of water to purge any sort of bloating, but that's it.

"The food is on its way and it shouldn't take long," he reassures when I don't answer him. "Don't worry."

I offer a jerky nod, thankful to change the subject. "Great. I'm starving." I'm also a liar. I can't eat around him. My stomach is tied up in knots just having him so close.

"Do you want to back out?" he suddenly asks, shocking me.

What brought that on?

No, I want to scream. What I want is to throw myself into his arms and beg him to kiss me. Feel those warm, soft lips settle on mine, the delicious, velvety hot glide of his tongue as he searches my mouth. I want to hear him whisper wicked words in my ear while his hands are sliding all over my body.

More than anything, I desperately want him to take off my clothes, push me to the bed, and have his way with me all night long.

But my wants are pointless. And ridiculous.

"Of course n—" I'm ready to tell him no, but he cuts me off.

"I know I'm being incredibly selfish, but I can't have you back out, Ivy. Still, I would never force you to do something you're not comfortable with."

His soft, beguiling tone warms me from within. When he looks at me like that, his dark gaze full of heat, his expression so sincere, I can almost believe him.

A knock sounds at the door, startling me. Irritation flashes in Archer's eyes at the interruption and I watch his long-legged stride eat up the floor as he heads toward the door. He throws it open, growls his greeting, and takes the cart from the hotel employee before the guy can push it inside.

I almost want to giggle, watching Archer pushing the cart laden with plates covered by silver domes into the room, as if he were the lowly employee and it isn't his family name on the outside of the building. "I hope you at least tipped him," I say.

His gaze darkens when he looks up at me. "Of course I did. I'm not totally heartless."

I wish I had the balls to say, *Prove it.*

But I hold the words back.

Archer

"YOU'RE STAYING HERE with me tonight."

I don't bother asking after I downed my third slice of pizza prepared by the hotel's gourmet chef. She's staying with me whether she likes it or not.

We're sitting in the dining area of the suite. The table is small, giving me the perfect excuse to sit close to her. Her scent lingers in the air, the warmth of her presence easing my earlier tension despite her obvious reluctance to come here.

And her obvious reluctance to agree to my plan. I know she still feels this way without her having to say a word. I can read her. I've always been able to.

Ivy picks at her food. "You're kidding, right?"

Christ. The woman throws up roadblocks every chance she can get. "Hell no, I'm not kidding. It's late.

I don't want to make the trek across town this time of night. You can stay in one of the other bedrooms. I swear I won't make a move." I scrub a hand across my cheek, my frustration mounting.

Clearly, Ivy has no plans on making this easy.

"Did you plan this too? Bringing me here tonight? Forcing me to stay?" Lifting her head, her gaze meets mine, her expression almost pained.

God, she exasperates me. "Of course I didn't."

"Seems like you did."

"Are we really going to go round and round about this?" I wipe my hands with a napkin, wad it up and throw it on my plate. "You hardly ate."

She shrugs. "I wasn't that hungry."

"So your growling stomach lied? I ordered all of your favorite foods." She used to gorge herself on junk when she was a teen. We all did. Hell, I still do. I also work out like crazy, so I can afford the occasional indulgence.

A sigh escapes her. "I haven't eaten this type of food in years."

"You used to."

"Back when I was a teenager and didn't need to watch everything I eat," she retorts, irritation flaring in her eyes.

I let my gaze slide over her. Damn, she's hot. With a killer bod and curves in all the right places. Places I wish I could explore again with my hands. Or even better, explore with my mouth. "One night isn't going to kill you, Ivy." I'm trying to tempt her, since all she has to do is sit there. I'm beyond tempted to jump her and show her how much I need her.

But not yet. I have to be patient, even if it kills me.

"I'll have to run extra hard if I bother eating one of those mozzarella sticks." She eyes the plate I specifically ordered for her, her tongue darting out to lick her upper lip. They'd been a weakness in her past.

"You run?"

"On a treadmill. At the gym." She shrugs.

"Come on, live a little." I push the plate toward her.

"Are you going to taunt me like this the entire two weeks we're together?" She arches a brow and I smile at her in answer.

I don't want her scared of me. Or worse, angry.

She plucks the mozzarella stick from her plate, dunks it in ranch dressing and takes a huge bite. Watching her eat pleases me for some weird reason. Pleases me even more that she spoke about our being together in a positive light.

"You deserve to cut loose and have a little fun every once in a while, you know. All work and no play makes Ivy a dull girl."

Ivy glares at me. Damn, she's pretty when she's angry. "Life isn't all fun and games." She takes another bite of the cheese stick, a little moan escaping her as she chews.

The sound sends a swift bolt of lust straight to my groin. "Isn't that the damn truth," I mutter.

"You certainly make it look that way though. Always out with two or three women hanging off your arm, drinking and having fun out at clubs all over town," she points out.

Hell, she thinks I'm a complete jackass. Especially with the way I've ignored her since we were last together.

If she only knew the truth. How difficult that had been, how much she scared me. How much she *still* scares me. "You really think all I've done is fuck around and spend my family's money these last few years?"

"Of course not." She pops the last of the mozzarella stick into her mouth, chews and then swallows. "Gage has told me how hard you work."

"And maybe you need to learn how to let loose more and have a good time," I return. Here we go, returning to our standard argumentative selves. I swear it's like foreplay between us. It masks all that sexual tension that's constantly brewing whenever we're together.

"I know how to let loose." Her voice is defensive.

"Then prove it." I am practically daring her. She's always worried over what everyone thought of her, ever since I've known her. Cultivating a certain image, not allowing anyone too close for fear they might see the real Ivy.

Not that there's anything wrong with the real Ivy. In my eyes, she's damn near the perfect woman.

"How can I prove it to you?"

I can't answer her for fear I'll say something so incredibly stupid, I'll fuck it all up.

I can't chance it. Too risky.

"Can I be honest?" she asks suddenly, shocking me from my thoughts.

"Please. By all means."

She watches me, her gaze direct, her expression serious, and I want to squirm. "You scare me."

Great. The feeling's mutual. "I won't do anything you don't want me to."

"That's not what I'm scared of." She exhales loudly. "Just being in your presence is like going on an exhilarating roller coaster ride, and I'm constantly terrified I might fall off and plunge to my death at any moment."

"Well. That sounds . . ."

"Pretty scary, right?" She smiles, though it doesn't quite reach her eyes. "I want to help you, Archer. I really do."

"Then quit waffling," I say vehemently. Fuck, I swear I'm losing her. She's slipping right out of my grasp like tiny granules of sand, and I can't do anything to stop it from happening.

"I've already agreed to help you. I don't have a choice but to agree, what with the way you handled this." She pauses, her tongue sneaking out to wet her lips. My heart lurches at the sight of her pretty pink tongue. "I'll help you, if you help me."

Relief floods me, leaving me weak. "Anything. I'll do anything you want. Name it and it's yours."

Ivy jerks her gaze from mine and bends her head, studying the table. "When we were . . . together last time. The night of Jeff and Cecily's wedding. It was good between us. Right?"

Uneasiness slips over me, sending a chill racing down my spine. Where is she going with this? "Yeah."

"So, what if we worked together and spent time together as if we were a real couple?" She keeps her head bent, sketching invisible doodles on the tabletop with her index finger.

"What do you mean?" Lusty hope rises within me. She couldn't be asking for what I think she is . . .

No way. This is Ivy. She wouldn't be so bold as to ask me to have a fling with her, would she?

I'd say yes. I'd get her any way I could, just to be with her.

"I want to spend more time with you, Archer. I want to get to know you. The adult you, not the rude teenager from our past." She shrugs those slim shoulders of hers, her voice sounding downright hopeless. "Over the years, we've grown apart, moved on with our lives. Having you back in my life makes me realize I've missed you."

Disbelief fills me. That she could be so honest, so incredibly forthright in what she wants from me is shocking. Normally I'm the brutally honest one. But Ivy changes everything. I would've hemmed and hawed and wondered how the hell I might approach her.

Hell, I'm doing that very thing right now. Yet she comes right out and asks for what she wants from me. I can't help but admire her for that.

"I've missed you too," I admit because she deserves those words. She jerks her head up, her wide-eyed gaze meeting mine, and I smile at her. "I thought you hated me."

"I do." She returns the smile. "But there's more between us than fights and hate and constant irritation. Don't you think?"

Oh, I know. But I'm not sure if I'm brave enough to tell her yet. Scrubbing a hand over my face, I'm half tempted to ask her why she's here. With me. I flat out don't deserve her.

"Yeah," I murmur, not sure what else I can say. I'm shocked she's willing to give me—us—another chance.

"But it'll be temporary. Once Crave's design is complete, we're finished. I'm sure you'll be ready to move on by then anyway." Her smile turns unnaturally bright. "From everything."

Not true. I'm ready to deny it, but she cuts me off.

"We walked away from each other before and you never called. I guess I could've called you but I don't operate like that." Her smile becomes more brittle and I'm tempted to lunge for her. Tell her exactly how much I want her and watch the wariness leave her gaze. And become replaced with pleasure.

And of course she doesn't operate like that. She's a traditional sort of woman who deserves a man who will chase after her without fear and make her his forever.

I suddenly want to be that sort of man. Only for Ivy though.

Not for anyone else.

"This is so embarrassing." She sighs and drops her head, keeps her gaze focused on the table in front of her. "The guys I've been with, they were all hopeless, you know? I wanted to fix them and they definitely didn't want to be fixed. And I get you don't want to be either. You're perfectly happy in your broken, messed-up state. But you, Archer, you were the first one I truly felt comfortable with. Like I could finally let go and . . ."

"And what?" I prod.

"Have an . . ." Her voice trails off again and her cheeks are pink. "You know."

Pride fills me even though I know it's a jackass move. But what man doesn't want to hear those words slip from the lips of a woman he's attracted to? "Have an orgasm?"

"Yeah." She gives a jerky nod. "They don't usually happen easily for me."

Well, hell. I have to help her. Prove to her she's a beautiful, desirable woman who deserves to have as many orgasms as she damn well pleases. Let her know just how much she undoes me with only a look. A smile. A glimpse of skin, a brief hug. Everything about her screams "take me", and my body is more than willing to do just that.

Clearing my throat, I decide to get down to business. After all, I'm a world-class negotiator. "So you want me to help you."

"Yes." She bites her lower lip, her expression full of worry.

"Have plenty of orgasms." This turn of events is downright surreal.

I'm not complaining.

Her cheeks color a pretty pink. "Yes."

"And in return, you'll help me."

She nods, not saying a word. "I still can't believe you want me for the project."

I roll my eyes in answer. "I can't believe you doubt your abilities."

"It's not that. It's just . . ."

"What?"

"I don't understand why you want me around," she whispers. "What's happening between us, Archer? It's confusing."

My heart lurches. I feel the same exact way. "I'm confused too, Ivy."

"You don't act like it. You're the usual smug, arrogant Archer."

"Deep inside, I'm petrified you'll tell me to fuck off." Couldn't she see that? I hardly uttered a word for the last five minutes. I just let her do all the talking.

She laughs, the tension easing from her expression at my confession. "I would never say that to you."

"Never say never."

"So we're in agreement then," she says, releasing a shuddering breath.

"Design skills for orgasms? I think so." I grin and she glares at me.

"You make it sound sleazy. You're paying me for my design skills." Worry flits through her gaze. "Right?"

I chuckle. "Of course. You know this." Pausing, I contemplate her. "But you don't have to pay me for the orgasms, you know. I'll handle that task for free. Gladly."

"Oh my God, this is the most embarrassing thing ever. I should've never told you." She buries her face in her hands.

I stand and slowly start to approach her. "Don't be embarrassed." My voice is soft and I stop directly in front of where she's sitting. "I'm glad you were honest with me."

She tilts her head back, her gaze meeting mine. "Will you be honest with me?"

I think of the bet. I think of Matt laughing his ass off at me. Of me owing him that extra fifty grand because damn it, he was right. I think of Gage wanting to murder me for defiling his sister.

"I'll try my best," I say because it's all I can offer.

"That works," she murmurs, a smile teasing the corners of her mouth. "I'm excited to see the new resort."

"I'm excited to show you."

"Calistoga is gorgeous."

"I agree. Wait till you see it. Hopefully you'll think the hotel is gorgeous too."

She nibbles on her lower lip, looking unsure and incredibly sexy. "I want to thank you for the opportunity. Letting me work with you," she says softly.

"I'm grateful you're willing to help." Reaching out, I skim my hand over the top of her head, my fingers tangling in the silky soft strands of her hair.

"Like I said, you really didn't give me any choice." She shakes her head, but I don't remove my hand. I never want to stop touching her. "I hope I don't disappoint you."

"You could never, ever disappointment me," I tell her, knowing I'm one hundred percent right. Though I'm starting to wonder if she's talking about disappointing me in a non-work-related way.

Again, she could never, ever disappointment there either.

"I don't know about that," she says, her voice full of doubt as she watches me approach.

"Let me prove it to you." I take her hand so I can pull her to her feet.

"How?" Her voice is trembling, her gaze meeting mine expectantly.

"Like this."

Chapter Twelve

Ivy

ARCHER'S MOUTH SETTLES on mine before I can utter a single word, and I'm completely lost. In the taste of him, the scent of him, the way he moves into me as if it's his every right to be there. Touching me, holding me, drawing me close, his arms circling my waist.

This is what I really want. Working with him will be a great boost to my career; the Bancroft Corporation a stellar client to put into my portfolio and an opportunity that I would be a fool to pass up.

But this is what I not-so-secretly crave. Being in Archer's arms again, his persuasive lips caressing mine, gently encouraging me to open to him. I do so easily, letting the soft sigh escape when his tongue touches mine. After all my arguments and protests, I still can't believe I confessed to him what I really wanted.

A chance to be with him, to lose myself with him. Freely.

He's the only one who's able to coax an orgasm out of me. Men have tried numerous times before with a variety of methods. And when it wouldn't work, when I didn't work, they made me feel like a freak. A few had even declared me frigid. Unresponsive. Unfeeling.

Jerks. They'd tried to tear down my self-esteem and for a while, I let them. Until I realized I didn't need any of them to give me an orgasm. I was fully in charge of that task. Quite happily, I might add.

Until Archer. And then *bam*. Instant orgasm. I'd like to experience that again.

And again and again and again.

"I've missed you," he whispers against my lips, his husky voice sending a scattering of gooseflesh across my skin. "So damn much, Ivy."

I'm about to tell him I missed him too, but he's kissing me again, more forcefully this time. His tongue strokes mine, his hands clutch at my waist, and I step into him, run my hands up his chest, my fingers molding to the wall of hot, firm muscle beneath my palms. He shivers from my touch, and I realize he enjoys my touch as much as I enjoy his.

Such a powerful, overwhelming discovery.

As our hands move, our lips search, the kiss becoming deep. Hot. I slide my tongue into his mouth and I rest my hands at his sides, my fingers slipping beneath his sweater so I can touch the smooth, bare skin of his back. He grips my waist, guiding me backward, until I'm bumping against the wall and he's got me trapped. Deliciously, wonderfully trapped.

He toys with the tie at the waist of my dress, his fingers playing with the ends, and then he's tugging. Pulling the tie undone until my dress loosens and he's pushing either side of it wide, exposing me to his perusal.

Breaking the kiss, he studies me, his smoldering gaze raking over my body, making me aware of how on display I am for him. I thrust my chest out and let him look his fill. Remind him of what he's missed out on for the last month.

Me.

"You're killing me." He slips his fingers beneath the strap of my black bra, moving to trace the scalloped lacy edge across one breast, then the other. "So fucking beautiful."

Pleasure swarms me, making me dizzy, and I lock my knees for fear I'll collapse. I almost cry out when he leans in, one hand braced on the wall beside my head, his mouth at my throat, then my collarbone. Dropping sweet little kisses on my chest, the tops of my breasts, sampling me. I grip his hips, holding on to him for dear life as he licks and kisses my skin.

Everything he's doing feels so good I'm afraid I might pass out from the pleasure of it all. My belly clenches, between my legs I grow hot and damp, and I bite my lip when he trails his fingers down my stomach until they're toying with the waistband of my matching black panties.

"I can see through them," he whispers, and I crack my eyes open to find his dark head bent, no doubt staring intently at the tiny scrap of material that's barely covering me. "I really think you are trying to kill me."

A soft burst of laughter escapes me and he glances up, a sexy smile curving his delicious lips. Tilting my head back, I brush my mouth with his, licking his lips, a soft moan escaping me when his tongue touches mine. I could get drunk off his kisses. His fingers are teasing me, sliding across my stomach, dipping just beneath the waistband of my flimsy panties, not quite reaching where I really want him to be.

"I think I'm going to enjoy this orgasm task," he mutters against my mouth, making me laugh again. I love how blunt he is. How honest. Spending time with him is never, ever boring.

Especially now.

"Let's take this off," he murmurs, pushing my dress off my shoulders so it falls to the crook of my arms. I straighten them as he steps away and the dress flutters to the ground in a heap around my feet. I kick the fabric away, standing before him in just my panties and bra and my black heels.

His gaze drops, running up the length of my body, frank appreciation in his eyes. "Holy hell, woman."

I feel hot from his words, the way he's looking at me. Thrusting my chest out farther, I contemplate him, heat blooming between my legs when he studies my breasts, no doubt seeing my nipples poke against the thin fabric of my bra.

Without warning he's on me, his mouth fused with mine, his hands cupping my breasts, thumbs circling my nipples. I arch into his touch, a long agonized groan escaping me when he tugs on my nipples. The pleasurable pain shoots through me, landing between my legs, and I rub against his thigh, sparks of heat blistering through me.

"I want to fuck you right here. Against the wall." His hand sinks into the front of my panties, finally touching me exactly where I want him. "So wet, Ivy. *God*."

He sounds tortured. I *feel* tortured. Without thought I grab him, mold my hand around the length of his erection, stroking him over his jeans. I wish I could touch his bare skin. I wish I could go down on my knees and draw him into my mouth . . .

Deciding that's the perfect idea, I frantically undo the snap and zipper on his jeans, shoving them down with impatient, shaky hands. They fall to his feet and he kicks them off, his mouth locked with mine once again, his hand between my legs. I ride that hand unashamedly, whimpering as his fingers work a sort of magic over me, and I lose myself in the sensation. My breaths leave me in shuddery exhales and I throw my head back, my eyelids fluttering as his fingers circle and stroke my clit again and again.

"Come for me, baby," he whispers against my lips just before he kisses me. "Reach for it."

A ragged little cry escapes me and I close my eyes, moaning when I feel his lips on the side of my neck. He drags his hot tongue over my skin as I grind against his palm and I'm close. So, so close, I'm almost afraid it's not going to happen.

"I can feel you. Hot and clenching so tight around my finger. You want more, don't you Ivy?"

His hot words send me straight into oblivion. My body is racked with tremors as my orgasm pulses through me, taking me completely over the edge until all I can do is ride the wave. I grip his shoulders for fear I might collapse as he continues to stroke me, his fingers feather light and so gentle I almost want to weep at how amazing his touch feels.

God. He makes me fall apart with a few hot kisses and delicious touches like some sort of sexual miracle.

As I slowly come back down to earth, I realize he's still touching me, licking my collarbone, pressing up against me. I can feel his erection brush against my stomach, still covered by his boxer briefs, and I reach for him. Brush my fingers down the light trail of dark hair that lines a path from his navel downward. Sliding my hands beneath the waistband of his underwear, I touch bare, hard skin, my fingers curling around his length.

"Jesus, Ivy," he chokes out.

Smiling, I slide my back down the wall until I'm level with his cock. Slowly I tug his underwear down, revealing him to my gaze, and his erection springs out toward me almost eagerly.

I feel just as eager. Exhilarated. Reaching for him, I curl my fingers around the base of him and lean in, dropping a kiss on the tip. His agonized groan fuels me and I lick him, wrap my lips around just the head as I suck and work him deeper.

"Not like this," he gasps, tugging on me so hard I have no choice but to stand and face him again, my feet wobbly since I'm still wearing the damn heels. I'm about to kick them off when he rests his hand on my cheek, making me look up at him. "Keep the shoes on."

Archer

THIS IS MY every fantasy come to life. Ivy in my arms, spent from the orgasm I just gave her. Ivy kneeling in front of me, drawing me into her mouth, her enthusiastic tongue whipping me into such a frenzy I knew I wouldn't last long.

No way was I going to come too fast again. This time around, I want to make it last as long as possible. So I yank her to her feet and push impatiently at her tiny panties, wanting them off. Then I'm unsnapping her bra, watching her toss it to the floor before I'm on her again, nestled close, our mouths locked, our tongues dancing, my hands wandering.

We're both naked save for her heels and I pick her up, her legs automatically going around my waist, her pointy heels poking into my ass but I ignore the sharp pain. I press my cock against her, dying to plunge inside her.

Fuck. I need a condom first.

"I'm on the pill," she whispers as if she can read my mind, and I lean back to study her. Her lips are puffy from our frantic kisses and her hair is in wild disarray about her head. Red marks dot her neck from my mouth and her chest is flushed; her nipples so hard I'm tempted to suck one into my mouth right now and pull and tug with my lips until she's whimpering from the pleasure.

"Yeah, uh ... despite what you've heard, I'm clean.

I swear." I swallow hard, overwhelmed with the idea of taking Ivy with no barriers. Just skin on skin. All that wet, silky heat sucking me deep . . .

"I want you, Archer." She tightens her legs around my hips and I can feel her. Hot. Slick. Tempting me like no one else ever has. "I trust you."

Her simple statement threatens to unravel me.

Reaching between us, I guide myself in, teasing her with the head of my cock before I finally sink into her depths. She throws her head back against the wall with a loud groan when I fill her completely and then we're moving. Grinding. We're in absolute perfect sync as she slowly rides the length of my cock.

Closing my eyes, I press my forehead to hers, breathing hard, trying to keep my shit together. She feels fucking amazing, surrounding me, all over me until she's the only thing I can see, hear, smell, taste. I turn my head and bite along her neck, soothing the nips with little flicks of my tongue, and she releases a shuddering sigh, my name falling from her lips.

That little sigh spurs me on, and I increase my pace. Her arms and legs clutch me close and I nuzzle her damp hair, breathe in her heady scent. I've never felt closer to a woman than I do at this very moment with Ivy. She's all I want. All I'll ever want.

The realization is so staggering I fumble for a moment, my hands gripping her ass tight. I pause, trying to keep my control, desperate to make this good for her, but she's circling her hips and sending me deeper. So much deeper I'm afraid I'll never find my way out of her.

"Harder, Archer," she breathes against my ear, making me shiver. "I want to come with you inside me."

Ah hell, she's as good of a tease as I am. Increasing my pace once more, I fuck her hard against that wall, her body thumping loud with my every thrust, our sweaty skin clinging to each other, my hand tangled in her hair as I grip the back of her neck and bring her in for a kiss. Our lips meet, our tongues stroke, and then I'm groaning against her, coming so fucking hard I swear I see stars.

She's coming too. I can feel her clench all around me, milking my orgasm further until I'm absolutely spent. We stand together for long, quiet moments, the only sounds our stuttering breaths, our frantic heartbeats. I'm not ready to let go of her yet, not ready to slip out of her hot depths and I stay there. Wrapped tight in her embrace, never ever wanting to move again.

"I ... uh. Wow," she murmurs minutes later, and I chuckle as I lift my head away from her to meet her gaze. "That was ... I didn't mean for that to happen."

"Really?" I kiss her, not insulted in the least. I don't doubt for a second she didn't mean for that to happen. I really didn't either.

But when she's sitting there talking about her lack of orgasms, it was like she threw down a challenge. I had to prove to her that she was wrong.

Did I ever.

"I just ..." She laughs and shakes her head. "You make it hard for me to form words, after all that."

"Mmm." I kiss her again, her swollen lips parting for

me easily as I search her mouth with my tongue. "We're amazing together."

"We are, aren't we?"

"I'm going to enjoy showing you just how amazing again and again over these next two weeks." I say it like a promise. A vow. Because it is.

She presses against my chest with her hands so I move away from her, but I still don't let her go. "That sounds promising."

I meet her gaze, schooling my expression, needing her to know the truth. "I was an idiot for pretending what happened between us didn't exist. And I'm sorry about that." Leaning in, I drop a soft kiss on her swollen lips. "I'm sorry I let you down. I can't wait to start working with you. I trust your instincts. I believe in your skills. And I can't wait for us to work together on this project and make my resort the best fucking thing the entire industry has ever seen."

A slow, sexy smile curves her lips and she kisses me again. "I love it when you talk like that."

"What, like an arrogant asshole?"

"Yes." Her lips linger on mine. "I find your arrogance . . . arousing."

"Really?" I'm doubtful, but I'll go with it.

"Yes. Really." She licks my cheek and I flinch. What the hell was that for? "Take me to bed, Archer. Show me what else those magic hands and fingers can do."

"Wait until you see what my magic tongue can do for you." I get hard just thinking about it.

"I can't wait to see."

Chapter Thirteen

Ivy

ELEVEN DAYS. I'VE been in Calistoga with Archer for eleven days and I can't believe how wonderful it's been. Busy and tiring and exhausting but also ... freaking amazing.

I don't ever want to come down off this high.

We've been working nonstop on Crave. It's small and quaint and gorgeous and sophisticated all at once. I've poured over endless fabric swatches, paint colors for the interiors, and searched through enough furniture catalogs and websites to make my eyes cross until I finally came up with the perfect color scheme for all eight of the suites, plus the lobby and spa accommodations.

All with Archer's approval, of course, and he's loved everything I've come up with. Considering we have similar taste, it's been a relatively easy road. For all our arguing and fighting from the past, it's hard for me to believe just how easily and well we work together. He's brilliant and smart and comes up with the best ideas. I constantly compliment him as if I can't help myself.

And then he thanks me by kissing me stupid, stripping me naked and having his way with me. Again and again and again.

Every night that we're together it's like this. We come together in a frenzy of heated breaths, delicious kisses, soft sighs, and wandering hands over naked skin. During the day we're on our best behavior, working hard, going over plans, all sorts of plans, or returning to Hush where Archer has to take care of his day-to-day responsibilities, which are tedious and sometimes irritating, but he always handles them with ease.

He's so good at his job, it's a joy to watch him in action. I admire the easy way he has with people. How efficiently he handles a guest complaint, an employee complaint, a call from some reporter inquiring about the Calistoga location. It's nonstop, everything he has to do.

As each day passes, my admiration for him grows. I care for Archer far more than I want to admit. I think he cares for me too. Spending so much one-on-one time with this gorgeous, frustrating, adorable, volatile, sweet, stubborn man, I can't get over how much I didn't know about him until now.

His drive. His passion. His intelligence. He so believes in what he's doing, the service he provides for people, he will do everything he can to ensure that he offers his guests the absolute best service their money can buy. And he's pulling out all the stops for the new resort. It's costing him a fortune. He'll charge his guests a fortune too. But I have a sneaking suspicion they'll love it and come back for more.

And he'll become an absolute success all over again.

Running my fingers through my hair, I scratch the back of my head, squinting at my laptop's screen. I've been searching for the lobby rugs and I can't find them. I have a visual in my head, but so far nothing comes close to my imagination. I'm afraid I'm going to have to settle.

I know if I told Archer that, he would flip. Demand I continue my search until I find rugs I absolutely love. He's definitely not about settling, even for rugs.

Hunched over my laptop, I curl my leg beneath me on the chair and sigh, scrolling through yet another textiles website, looking through a ton of ugly rugs that are all wrong, no matter how much I try to make them right. My vision is blurry and my neck aches. It's past seven, I'm so ready to call it quits but I'm trying to wait for Archer to return.

Silly, yes, but I can't help myself. I want to see him.

When we're not in Calistoga, we're headquartered in Archer's office at Hush. That's where I'm at now, waiting for him while he handles some sort of urgent issue. There are always urgent issues for Archer to handle. He does everything at Hush. The man has so much on his plate it overwhelms me, and I'm not the one who has to take care of it all; I'm only an observer. Most of the time he's putting out various fires, which must get super old.

But I guess this is what comes with being the owner.

Stretching my arms above my head I grimace when I hear and feel my neck pop, then settle back into position. I curl my fingers around the mouse when big, warm hands settle on my shoulders, making me yelp in surprise.

"So tense," Archer murmurs, his deep voice sounding directly in my ear.

"You scared the crap out of me." I sink my teeth into my lower lip when he starts to rub to keep a moan from escaping. Oh my God, that feels so good. I think I might melt into a pool of nothing if he keeps it up.

"Sorry. You were too busy scowling at your laptop." He continues to massage my shoulders and I close my eyes, savoring his touch. How good he makes me feel. "Find what you want?"

If we're talking about you, yes I sure did. "Not really," I admit with a sigh.

He's standing directly behind my chair, rubbing my shoulders, his fingers digging into my flesh. My entire body warms and loosens at having his hands on me and I want to turn around, grab him, and tell him let's go back home.

Scary, how I'm starting to think of his house as home. I'm certainly not spending my nights in the guest room, that's for sure. Or at Hush like we'd originally planned. No, I get to spend them in his amazing, humongous bed in his equally amazing, humongous master bedroom.

The man certainly knows how to live with every luxury available. My parents may be wealthy, but they're downright modest compared to Archer.

"You should schedule a massage," he murmurs, dropping a kiss on top of my head.

My insides warm at the sweet gesture. I'm dying to have that mouth of his on mine. "Why would I need to when I have you?" Opening my eyes, I heave a big sigh. Yes. Yes, I've lost it. All over Archer.

All for Archer.

"True." He sounds amused, his voice warm, his touch gentle as he squeezes my shoulders. "I'll give you a more thorough massage when we get home."

"I like the sound of that."

"It'll involve special oils from the spa and you completely naked." His voice drops to a husky whisper, sending shivers down my spine, and I smile at my laptop screen.

"Sounds absolutely amazing."

"It will be, I can promise you that." He crouches beside me, his face level with mine, and I cut my gaze to his, marveling at his handsome features. His dark brown hair falls across his forehead, making me want to reach across and push it away. So I do, my fingers sifting through the silky soft strands. "Still looking for rugs for the lobby, huh?"

"It's been a rather ... frustrating process." I click out of the website I was perusing and turn more fully to face him.

"I know someone who designs rugs. Has a studio where they're hand woven." He smiles. "Every one of them is like a work of art."

"I'm sure they are. Very expensive works of art," I stress. We're completely over budget but he flat out doesn't care. He spares no expense. It sort of drives me crazy.

And makes me admire him even more.

He shakes his head. "I've never seen a person so obsessed with rugs before."

"That's because I have an idea in my head I can't shake." I tap my forehead. "And it sucks because I'm forever disappointed in every stupid rug I see."

"That does it. I'm calling her right now and we'll make an appointment to see her tomorrow. She can create whatever you want, she's that good." He whips out his phone and starts scrolling through his contacts. "Actually, I'll text her, see if she's available in the morning."

"Archer, we only have a few days until we're open. No way can she get them done in time." I shake my head, shocked he would go to such lengths to please me.

"Then we'll throw some solid color rugs out for a few days to cover while I insist she rush the process. Trust me, they'll work on the rugs twenty-four-seven if I pay her right."

"They're not worth that much . . ." I start, but he silences me with a look that I find so incredibly sweet and sexy I feel my heart crack a little more every time I see it.

Like right now. It's cracking wide open, all for Archer.

"If it makes you happy, it's worth it. You've already sketched out what you wanted for me, remember?"

I nod, a little embarrassed that we're having this discussion over freaking rugs. "That you're willing to go to such lengths over something you don't know what it's going to look like says a lot."

"Like I'm crazy?" His smile grows, that dimple of his flashing and I lean in, giving it a kiss.

"I'm the crazy one." *Crazy for you* . . .

Just thinking that freaks me out a little.

"Yeah, you are, baby," he drawls. I love it when he calls me baby. My stomach flutters as he leans in closer, and I can make out every speck of stubble on his cheeks, see the tiredness in his dark brown eyes. He looks as exhausted as I feel and I have the sudden urge to comfort him.

"You're definitely crazy though," I say, entranced with the gold flecks in his brown eyes, the way they look at me full of so much emotion. Emotion I can't quite figure out but I don't want to. It's a little scary to contemplate, and I'm not ready to face it yet. "You're drastically over budget."

"You're the one who put the budget on me. The sky's the limit for this place. I already told you that." He kisses me, his lips lingering, and just like that I want him.

He makes me want to lose all control . . . and gladly.

Pulling back, I roll my eyes. The budget I tried to get him to agree to has flown right out the window. No wonder he drives his father crazy. Don Bancroft plans and plots to the finest detail. He has a list and a chart and a spreadsheet for every little thing. He doesn't go a penny over budget unless he's absolutely forced to, at least according to the stories my brother told me. And when he does go over budget, he's grumbling and griping the entire time.

Whereas Archer tends to fly by the seat of his pants and hope like hell it all comes together. It worked for him before with Hush. I know it's going to work this time around too with Crave. I can feel it. His love and excitement for this opening far outshines anything else.

Well, his excitement for me is pretty shiny too. Love? Yeah, I doubt that, but I'm going to revel in what we share while we have it. Because it's fleeting, I know this.

I think he knows it too.

Our two weeks together are almost up, and I can hardly stand the thought of being away from him.

"We shouldn't have your friend make those rugs. I'm sure I can find something that'll work. I like the solid color idea. It's simple. Won't put me through so much torture while I look for the perfect pattern. Now I just need to find the perfect color." I turn away from him, my finger poised to resume scrolling, and he touches my arm, causing me to look at him again.

"I already texted her. We'll meet with her tomorrow first thing. Your work day is officially over." He smiles, softening his demanding words. "I'll take you to dinner if you'd like."

"Where?" I ask breathlessly, my arm tingling from his touch. His palm is wide, his fingers long, and he's smoothing his hand up and down my arm, making my breath come a little quicker. "I'm kinda tired. It's been a long day."

"We could stay here tonight. There are a couple of suites available. We could order room service, maybe?" He raises his brows, waiting for my answer.

I've wanted to try out those outdoor bathtubs built for two since I first saw one. Working with Archer has turned into a kind of torturous foreplay, one I both delight and agonize in. All the wanting and the yearning throughout the day, the lingering glances and the quick touches.

Archer Bancroft makes me feel like a confident, smart, and desirable woman. And I'm going to wield my newfound power on the very man who gave it to me.

Archer

"Room service sounds perfect," Ivy says after a too long pause. Hell, for a minute there I thought she was going to say no.

It was slow at Hush, which worked out in my favor since I spent half of my time in Calistoga lately. Always with Ivy by my side, helping me, offering her suggestions, guiding me when I went off track, me pushing her when she was being too conservative.

First day in, I realized pretty quickly we make a good team. There are enough differences between us which balance our personalities and allow us to work well together. Hard to notice when in the past, all we ever did was argue every time we came together.

But the arguing was a result of all that troublesome sexual attraction getting in the way. Not that it's disappeared. Hell no. But we're taking care of that issue every single night. We're both exhausted after a heavy and long workday, but we always make time for each other. In bed. Wrapped around each other, naked limbs entangled. My ultimate task of the day is making Ivy moan with pleasure.

I'm falling for her. Hard. Fast. I don't want her to leave. She feels like a true partner in every sense of the word.

That scares the shit out of me.

Working side by side with Ivy since she came here has been exhilarating. Getting to know her, watching her in her element has left me impressed. She may be young and at an early point in her career, but she's smart and instinctive, with excellent taste. Without a doubt, I know my resort is going to look unbelievable when we're finished.

I just hope we can wrap it all up and have it ready in the next few days. That's the only thing making me anxious.

Well, that and the fact that as soon as Crave opens, Ivy's gone. Out of my life.

Fuck, that fills me with so much despair I can barely stand thinking about it. She doesn't think I'll stick. And sometimes I doubt myself too. I don't want to subject her or myself to a relationship that's doomed to fail.

But are we really doomed? I don't know. I'm so used to thinking that way, it's hard to believe anything else.

"So you want to get a room? Or eat here in the office then head on home?" I definitely don't want the formality of my office this evening, eating at my desk, talking business like we've been doing constantly since I've brought her here.

I want to be in a suite tonight, alone with her and shut off from the rest of the world. We can eat, plan our schedule for tomorrow, and then indulge in each other. My favorite part of the day is the nights. Being alone with Ivy.

Being inside Ivy.

How will I feel, though, when it's all over? Normally, with women, it's never an issue. Hell, I don't allow women to become this close to me ever. Their expectations grow to insurmountable proportions, and I'm left fending off their disappointment and sense of abandonment.

I have this feeling that with Ivy, it will become difficult to let her out of my sight, let alone out of my life. I'll be the one with the sense of abandonment when she leaves me.

"How about I call the order in and you go get us a suite?" I suggest.

She smiles, her hazel eyes sparkling. When she looks at me like that, I feel ten feet tall and like I can do no wrong. It's too easy, what we share.

I remember complaining to Gage that it made me nervous when things were too easy. I should be feeling that way at this very moment.

But all I can do is think about how pretty she is. How much I want to kiss her. How I enjoy spending every waking moment with her. Every sleeping moment with her too.

"Sounds perfect. I've been wanting to try one of those outdoor bathtubs, you know," she admits coyly. "Do you want me to order for you? I love how the menu is always changing."

That's because I hired a world-class chef who's a pain in my ass and worth every penny I pay him. "Yeah, order me something. You know what I like. I'll come find you in about ten minutes, okay? I have a few things I need to wrap up first."

"All right." Shutting her laptop, she stands and I grab her, pulling her into my arms. She turns more fully into me, her gaze meeting mine, eyes large and unreadable as she grips my tie and pulls me in for a kiss. I bury my hands in her hair, messing it up completely, not giving a shit. I love it when she's messy and looking dazed, her cheeks flushed, her lips swollen from our constant kissing.

Damn it, I have it bad for this woman. And I don't really care if anyone knows it or not. Even Matt.

Even Gage.

Yeah, I need to tell Gage. They both need to know what's going on. Not that I'm coughing up the money, not yet. They said she didn't count, but damn it, she counts to me. But I won't be paying off any sort of bet until I put a ring on her finger.

I can't believe I'm contemplating putting a ring on Ivy's finger.

"I'll see you in a bit then?" she murmurs when I finally break the kiss. Her face is turned up to mine, her lips still slightly pursed, her lids heavy, giving her a sultry, sexy look. Her scent surrounds me, heady and sweet, and I'm tempted to jump her right here. Wouldn't be the first time we fucked around on top of my desk. Last time, I'd pushed her skirt up, tugged her panties aside, and made her come with just my tongue in record time. Had to, since there'd been a meeting I needed to attend and they were all waiting for me.

I'm getting hard just remembering it.

"Yeah, I'll be quick, I promise." I'm already anxious to see her and she hasn't even left yet. She smiles as if she can read my mind, and I lick my lips, staring at her mouth, ready to give in and kiss her again. She sways toward me, a little sigh leaving her as our mouths come closer, closer . . .

My fucking cell phone rings and I spring away from her,

running a hand through my hair, sending it into a haphazard mess. We've been rudely interrupted before, and I hate it. "Shit," I mutter as I pull it out of my pocket and see the number, watching as Ivy steps back, smoothing a few loose strands of hair behind her ear, nibbling on her lower lip.

Damn it, I wish I was the one nibbling on her lower lip.

"What the hell is going on with you and my sister?" Gage says. No hello, no what's up. Just launches right in with the diatribe.

"She's working for me, Gage. You already know this." I look at Ivy, who's pointing at the door and mouthing *See you later* before she dashes out of my office without another word.

Lucky her, she doesn't have to deal with her pissed-off brother.

"Yeah, but I saw some cozy picture of the two of you together. It looks like you're about to kiss her." Gage is literally yelling at me. "What the hell, man?"

"What picture are you talking about?" Oh. Shit. Who took a photo of us? And where? Do I have the paparazzi trailing my ass?

Of course I do. How easy I forget.

"I don't know. You guys are outside somewhere. You're standing real close and she's leaning into you. It seriously looks like the two of you are about to kiss or were just kissing." Gage pauses, takes an audible deep breath. "If you're with her, you better not break her heart. I'll fucking kill you, Archer, and you know it."

"I'm not with her," I automatically say, wincing the moment the words fall from my lips. I've turned into a liar.

Easy as that.

"So what's up with the picture? Oh yeah, and did I mention your arm is around her?"

Damn, did Gage withhold that bit of information on purpose?

"I have no idea. I'll admit, we've become closer. We spend a lot of time together working. And we're actually getting along. Can you believe it?" Nothing but silence on Gage's end, which of course makes me want to squirm. "There's nothing to worry about, Gage. I swear," I say as I walk around my office and gather up miscellaneous papers and whatever else is lying around, cleaning it up for the end of the night. I'm full of nervous energy, and I need to keep myself occupied before I bust out a *Fine-you-caught-me-I-think-I'm-falling-in-love-with-your-sister-tell-me-what-to-do* confession.

"Tell me you're not sleeping with her."

Well hell. Leave it up to Gage to get right to the point.

"I'm not sleeping with her," I automatically say because I'm not—not really. When I get Ivy in my bed, there's rarely any sleeping involved.

"Don't forget the bet," he reminds me, like I ever could. That bet is burned into my brain, making me feel like shit because if she ever finds out, especially now, she'll probably hang me by my balls and let Gage have his way with me. Not that I could blame her. I feel like a liar. Like I'm hiding the bet, hiding our relationship as if I'm ashamed to be seen with her. And that's definitely not the case. "And don't forget she's my goddamn sister."

"I'm not involved with Ivy," I mutter, falling into my

desk chair with a thump. Shit. I do not need this sort of lecture tonight. This is going to kill my mood for sure if I let it. And I'm already letting it. "She doesn't count, remember? You and Matt both said that."

I hate even saying it, let alone thinking it. She counts far more than I could ever imagine.

"Yeah, I know what we said, but she's still pretty and sweet and hell, for all I know you've wanted her for years. I have no clue." Damn, Gage's too close to the truth for comfort. He sounds worried and that makes me feel like hell.

Does he really think I'd be a ruthless jerk, going after his sister with no thought and callously hurting her? "She's a friend. She does her job well. You already knew this was going to happen when I called you a few weeks ago, remember?" How easy Gage forgets. I swear he's in his own little world. "Why the panic now?"

"I didn't think you'd actually ask her to work for you." He pauses. "And I've been . . . distracted. Not around much. I had no idea she wasn't even in town."

"Well, I did hire her and she's staying here with me. At the resort." Lies again, but damn, I don't want him knowing she's staying at my house. In my bed. "And she's doing a fantastic job." I lean back in my chair, glancing up at the ceiling. "Don't worry. Your sister is safe with me."

"She'd better be. Normally I don't trust you as far as I can throw you, but this is Ivy we're talking about. You hurt her, I hurt you."

I know without a doubt, Gage will make good on his promise.

Chapter Fourteen

Archer

Opening night.

"So what do you think?"

I turn to find Ivy standing in front of me, wearing a dress that should be outlawed, she looks so damn good in it. Too damn good. "Uh . . ." I can't find my tongue, and I nearly swallow it when she does a little twirl, the skirt flaring out to reveal her pretty knees, her slender thighs.

"I love it, but I don't know," she says when she's facing me once again, a giant smile on her face. Her hair is up, her elegant neck exposed, little tendrils of dark brown hair curling against her cheeks and neck. She's so beautiful it hurts to look at her. "Say something, Archer, before I think you hate it."

The dress is white lace and sleeveless, the neckline

dipping into a deep V that exposes all that smooth, kiss-able skin. A simple gold satin ribbon winds around her, just below her breasts, tied in a pretty bow at her back, and I'm tempted to slowly pull it undone. Unzip the dress, peel it off her, and kiss her everywhere.

But we have an opening party to go to for Crave. That we're already running late to.

"I think you look amazing." I go to her and drop a gentle kiss to her lips. She looks nervous and I grab her hands, giving them a squeeze. "What's wrong, baby?"

"What if they hate it?" she blurts out. "The interiors? All of it? I'll never be able to forgive myself."

"They're not going to hate it. Everything looks fuck-ing amazing." It does. She did a phenomenal job. We did a phenomenal job together. Proving to me yet again that we make a great team.

"Really?" She's looking at me, really looking at me, and I know she needs my reassurance now more than ever.

"Really." I kiss her again, this one a little longer, leav-ing her breathless when we break apart. "I wouldn't lie to you."

That in itself is a lie. I'm keeping something from her right now. Like that stupid bet. It's the most juvenile thing I've ever participated in, and I don't want her to hear what Matt and Gage had to say. How she didn't count. How none of them think I could possibly be interested in her.

I need to come clean before Gage or Matt ruin it and tell her first. They're both supposed to be attending to-night, but they won't get a chance to talk to her alone. I'll make sure and keep her by my side the entire evening.

"Archer . . ." She breathes deep, as if gathering strength, and I squeeze her closer, not wanting to break this physical or emotional connection we have. "What's going to happen after tonight?"

"What do you mean?" I know exactly what she means. I'm just stalling for time so I can come up with a logical answer.

"Between us. I—I have to go back home. I need to go back to my job." She drops her head, pressing her forehead into my chest, and I wrap my arms around her waist, holding her close. "I don't want to leave you," she whispers.

My heart constricts. This has happened so damn fast. And I let it. Enjoyed it, really. "I don't want you to leave either," I admit.

She sighs, and I feel all the tension leave her body as she melts against me. "You don't know how glad I am that you said that."

Slipping my hand beneath her chin, I tilt her face up, see the tears shimmering in her pretty hazel eyes. They're more green than brown at the moment and I kiss away the tear that drops on her cheek, my heart aching at seeing that physical display of emotion coming from her. "I'm falling in love with you, Ivy." I've already fallen. And there I went, fucking admitting it. What is wrong with me?

I'm in love with Ivy. That's what's wrong with me.

"Oh." She presses her lips together and closes her eyes, but another tear falls onto her cheek. I kiss that one away too. "God, Archer, I—I'm falling for you too."

She didn't say love, not that I'm going to hold it against her. For once, I'm laying it all on the line for a woman. For this woman—the woman I love. The woman I think I've always loved, I just never knew it until this very moment.

"We need to go, baby." I kiss her again, because after making such a confession from the deepest, darkest part of your soul, you have to be reassured your woman is on the same page.

The responsive way she kisses me, clings to me, tells me that yes, indeed, she is more than on the same page. We're writing the same damn book. Together.

"Can we talk later? Tomorrow? About . . . us?" she asks when I finally, reluctantly pull away from her.

"Whatever you want." I cup her cheek, staring into her eyes. Feeling myself fall more and more in love with her.

"I CAN'T BELIEVE how much you transformed this place." Matt glances around the lobby, his eyes wide as he drinks it all in. "It looks incredible, Archer. You should be proud, man."

I am. So damn proud, I feel like I'm going to burst. "Yeah, you saw it in its barest, ugliest, pared-down state, didn't you?"

It had been a dilapidated, falling-down-around-my-ears building that had once housed a premiere spa. Before the recession came along and took down the previous owner's business with a mighty, ugly fall. The building stood empty for about four years, allowing looters and whatever other bums came through to completely trash the place and gut it of anything valuable.

But I'd known from the moment I walked inside, it had potential. I'd purchased the building and land for pennies on the dollar. Best decision I ever made. Not only did I have a new business to be proud of, but creating this resort brought Ivy and me together.

"I sure did and I thought the place looked like something out of a horror movie. Might've tried to discourage you from buying it too, not that you would have listened to me. But you're the one with the vision, not me." Matt shook his head, his gaze still sweeping the interior. "And Ivy helped you with it all, huh?"

"Yeah, more like she chose everything. The furniture, the art that covers the walls, the light fixtures, the accessories, all of it is Ivy's vision, which complements mine, thank God. I just signed off on all the invoices and didn't bother arguing with her. Everything she chose totally works, don't you agree?" I want to hear him praise her. I need someone to join in with me, since I sound like an overeager boyfriend too proud of his woman.

Which I sort of am.

"I do agree. The place is gorgeous. And there was no arguing between you two, huh? That's rather unlike you and Ivy," Matt jokes.

"I know. We uh, work well together." Understatement of the year. Ivy and I do everything well together.

"I'm sure," Matt said wryly. "You got something going with her and hoping to hide it from us? Is that it?"

"Of course not," I retort, nerves eating at my gut. Ivy's

close by but out of earshot, and the last thing I want is for her to walk in on this conversation.

"You two looked pretty cozy to me when you first arrived."

We'd run a little late but still arrived before the start time of the party, so we hadn't expected any of our guests to be there yet.

It was just like Matt to screw it all up and actually show early. And witness Ivy and me walking into the lobby with my arm around her waist. Making her blush and giggle when I whisper how fucking sexy she looks.

Though Matt greeted each of us with an easy smile and a friendly hug, I felt the nerves radiating off of Ivy. I wonder if she could feel the nerves vibrating off me.

Most likely. We haven't been caught by the outside world yet. Well, not to her knowledge. I never told her about the picture Gage called me about.

"I'm not going to deny we've become closer," I finally say when I realize Matt is waiting for an explanation. "But we're just friends. There's nothing going on between us." Now why the hell did I say that?

"Really." Matt's voice is flat and clear of emotion. Meaning he doesn't believe a word I say.

"Really," I agree with a nod. "She's so damn talented though. You should consider hiring her when you redesign the winery's interior."

"Who said I was redesigning it?" Matt asked, looking slightly taken aback.

"Have you taken a look around the place? It could use some sprucing up. Bring in a more modern feel." The winery he recently purchased was dark and dreary, the furnishings in good condition but old. He needs a new look if he wants to make a splash amongst the many wineries in this area.

"Is she expensive? I'm sure that snob Sharon Paxton charges a fortune for use of Ivy's services," Matt mutters.

"She's worth it." I spot Ivy standing not a few feet away from us, talking with one of my Hush clients who I invited to see the new location. The opening party is small and intimate, much like the resort itself, and I invited only a select few to catch that first glimpse of Crave.

We'll open the suites in a week. A few finishing touches need to be made, but for the most part, Ivy's job is done. Though we're talking tomorrow, maybe even later tonight. If I have my say in any of this, she won't leave my side again. I want her to move in with me.

Gage is going to shit a brick. Matt is going to call me out on all the lies I'm telling him. But I don't care. Maybe I should just come clean right now. I want Ivy with me for the rest of my life, forget that stupid-ass bet. She's worth a million bucks. Hell, she's priceless to me.

"I'm sure you think she's worth every penny," Matt says, the amusement in his voice clear.

"I told her she should start her own design consulting business." I slip my hands into my suit pockets, my gaze locked on her as she walks away from the client, only to be stopped by one of the waitstaff who hands her a glass of champagne.

"I'll be her first client. Tell her if she's considering it, she needs to sign me up," Matt says. "She does fabulous work." He's looking at me again and I tear my gaze away from Ivy to find him smiling at me, looking infinitely entertained. "Nothing going on between the two of you, huh? Your eyes were eating her up just now. As if you know exactly what she looks like beneath that dress."

Asshole. Panic flares within me. I don't want to deal with this right now. "Where the hell is Gage anyway?" I ask, trying to change the subject.

"I don't know. He's been a hard fucker to pinpoint lately. I'm not sure what's up with him." Matt steps closer to me, his voice lowering. "Come on, Archer. Tell me the truth. I won't say anything to Gage. Are you and Ivy together?"

Guilt settles heavy on my chest. I can't talk about this here and now. I need to talk to Gage. Get his permission, convince him I won't do wrong by his sister. I love her. But I can't confess everything yet. Not here, not now.

"No," I say emphatically. "She's just Ivy, remember? She doesn't count." Even as I say the words, they don't feel right. She's not just Ivy. She's never been *just* anything.

Just the girl for me, but that's it. And that's enough.

"What did you say?"

Icy dread slithers down my spine as I turn to find her standing before me, her eyes wide, all the color drained from her face. Ah, hell, she heard me. "Hey baby," I start, but she cuts me off with a look.

"I want to hear you say it, Archer." Her voice is cold, her eyes hard, and my heart sinks. I'm in big-ass trouble. Damn it, I need her to listen to me. "Ivy, let me explain." But again she stops me, this time with a shake of her head.

"No. There's no need for an explanation. I heard exactly what you said. I don't count."

"You misunderstood me ..." I need to make this right, get to her to listen to me. Her expression is tight, her mouth so thin her lips practically disappear, and she's so rigid I fear she might shatter if I so much as touch her.

I don't dare try. She'd probably kick my ass, she looks that pissed. And I can't blame her.

Yet again, I fucked it up royally. I didn't even mean to.

"There's nothing to misunderstand. You said it yourself, Archer. I. Don't. Count." She takes a step toward me, throwing her hands out and shoving my chest so hard I have no choice but to take a staggering step backward. "I can't believe you. After everything I said earlier. After everything *you* said, then you deny what's happened between us to Matt like I don't matter. What an idiot I am to think we could actually have something together."

I'm losing her. Fuck, I can't lose her. Not like this. "Come on baby, let's talk about this somewhere else." If only I could get her alone, I could make this right. She needs to listen to me. Not in front of Matt and whoever else is nearby, listening in. Matt's watching us like we've both lost our minds and a few guests are lingering, trying to catch bits of our heated conversation, no doubt.

Shit. I'm not just losing the only woman who's ever really mattered to me all in a matter of minutes, I'm also making an ass of myself during Crave's opening night.

Feeling helpless, I try to grab her, but she yanks her arm out of my grip, her eyes wild and full of angry fire.

"Please, Ivy. I need to explain everything to you. Privately."

"I don't want to hear your explanations. They're worthless. Absolutely worthless. Just like whatever happened between us the last few weeks is worth nothing. I should've known it was all an illusion. That you would dismiss me so easily to Matt, I just ... I can't do this, Archer." She walks away, holding her head high, but I can see the wobble in her step. I hurt her so badly, I don't know if I'll ever be able to recover from this.

I wonder if she'll be able to recover from this. That she would jump to the conclusion that I don't care about her hurts too. After everything we've shared, she wouldn't even fucking listen to me.

It makes no sense.

"Well, you sure went and fucked that all up," Matt mutters as soon as she's gone.

"Shut up," I mumble. I can't just leave to go after her and it's killing me. This is my damn party. I have to be here to greet everyone and it's only started.

But I want to chase after her and explain. I need to explain. That she heard me say that ... breaks my fucking heart for her.

"Why didn't you just tell me the truth? I knew you were lying anyway," Matt says.

"So why did you keep on asking then?"

"Because I wanted to hear you admit it. I have to say, it made me happy for you, man, seeing you when you first walked in with Ivy. Your entire face lit up when you were staring at her, and she looked at you like you hung the damn moon." Matt shook his head. "Leave it to you to say something so stupid, you fuck up a good thing with two simple words."

Yeah. Leave it to me to fuck it all up with two words. Just Ivy.

The woman I'm in love with.

Just Ivy.

The woman I hurt.

The woman I failed.

Chapter Fifteen

Ivy

Two weeks later.

"WE'RE STILL ON for lunch, right?"

Sighing, I check my schedule and see that my lunch hour is completely free. How unfortunate. I've become so unsocial it's painful. "I don't know if I'm up to it, Wendy," I start, but she cuts me off with an irritated snort.

"Screw that business, girlfriend. I'm taking you out to lunch whether you like it or not. We're going to that sushi place you love, we're going to order not one but two of our favorite rolls and then we're going to devour them until we feel like we're going to burst. What do you say?"

Sounds like a nightmare. But I can't say that to Wendy. She's my best friend and she's only trying to cheer me up after that fiasco of a so-called relationship with Archer. "Fine. Want me to meet you there?"

"Yeah, if you don't mind. Say around twelve-thirty?"

"That should work." Luckily enough, Sharon doesn't mind if my lunch hour is flexible, as long as she can get a hold of me whenever she needs me. The more I've worked with her, the more I enjoy it.

She didn't ask questions about the Archer experience either. I forwarded her pictures for my online portfolio, she expressed her pleasure with the interior design I came up with, and that was that. Nothing else was said.

Just the way I prefer it. Talking about Archer—heck, even thinking his name—hurt too much.

"See you then." Wendy pauses, and I clutch the phone tight, scared of what she might say. "Chin up, okay hon? Don't let this get you down. He's just a man, after all."

"Right, just a man," I say weakly, wondering if she realizes she's mirroring the same hurtful thing he said about me.

Just Ivy . . . she doesn't count.

If he walked into the room right now, I'd probably slug him in that too-pretty face of his. Let's see if he would refer to me as *just Ivy* then.

God, I miss him. I want him back—I'm in love with him. But I can't forgive him for saying what he did to Matt. Doesn't help that I spoke to my brother, and he told me some story Archer had spun to him as well. Denying that we were together, swearing up and down nothing was going on be-tween us. Something about a picture Gage saw online of the two of us together, smiling at each other like we're in love.

Archer didn't bother to tell me about that picture either.

He lied to everyone. He lied to me. My heart still aches.

But would I ever get over him? I really, really hope so. Someday.

I throw myself into my work because it's the only thing that keeps my mind occupied and off my troubles. I move through my days like some sort of ghost. Functioning, able to complete my tasks, meet with clients, answer the phone, only to go home and crawl into bed. Watch sappy movies and cry into my pillow, wishing I wasn't alone.

I am a pitiful, horrible wreck.

In my sleep, he comes to me. Smiling that beautiful smile of his, the dimple flashing, and then I'm suddenly in his arms. Slowly melting when he whispers how much he loves me. Until I'm falling completely under his spell, ready for him to make love to me.

Then I wake up and realize it was all just a dream and I'm alone. Without him. I tell myself it's better this way. He would've hurt me sooner or later, and it was best that it happened sooner, no? Now it's out of the way, and I can move forward.

But my mind and my body are stuck in the past, still longing for Archer. I can't help it.

Not that it's been that long since the incident, as I refer to it. Less than two weeks, that's it. He's called. He's texted, but I refuse to answer him or talk to him. At least he hasn't called my work, or worse, my parents.

God, that would be mortifying. Bad enough he's

phoned Gage repeatedly, who calls him all sorts of vulgar names before he hangs up on him.

Gotta love a big brother who defends you no matter what, even against his best friend.

My desk phone rings, knocking me from my morose thoughts, and I pick it up, surprised to hear Sharon's voice. "Ivy, I have a huge favor to ask of you," she starts.

"Sure." I grab a pen, ready to take notes in case I need to. Sharon talks fast, and I feel like I'm constantly scribbling across a notepad when I talk to her in the hopes I'll remember what to do. "What's up?"

"I have a client coming by in fifteen minutes and there's no way I can be there in time to meet him. Could you do it for me? I hate to ask this of you but I don't have a choice. I'm stuck in traffic, and I already had a late start back to the office."

"Sure. Who are you meeting with?"

"Matthew DeLuca. Have you heard of him?"

"What? Of course I have. He and my brother are good friends." I'm in shock. Why would Matt want to meet with Sharon? Why wouldn't he meet with me? If this has anything to do with the winery, I'm almost offended. I heard rumors he was going to refurbish it. I totally wanted to check it out and see what exactly needs improving.

Not that I want to be in the same vicinity as Archer . . . do I?

Of course you do, you lovesick idiot.

"Well, perfect. Ought to be easy for you to talk to him and find out what he's looking for since you know him so well." She rattles a few other facts off to me before she hangs up. I settle the phone in its cradle, surprise still coursing through my veins.

Okay, now I'm irritated. Why didn't he reach out to me first? I'm so calling Matt and chewing him out for not wanting to meet with me.

Of course, seeing Matt will also remind me of Archer and that will hurt. It especially hurts because Matt was the one Archer said all of those horrible, hurtful things to about me. He witnessed our entire argument, the reason why we fell apart.

I hate that. But I'll need to face him sometime, so it may as well be sooner rather than later.

Within minutes I hear the front door buzzer. The entrance is kept locked during the day so we don't have any strange people busting in uninvited. I stand, smoothing my hands down my skirt as I exit my office and enter the lobby, only to stop short when I see who's standing on the other side of that door.

It's not Matt.

It's Archer.

Stiffening my spine, I stride toward the door, stopping just in front of it. "Go away," I tell him, knowing he can hear me.

He slowly shakes his head, looking so devastated, so sad, he's breaking my heart.

Stupid, too-soft heart.

"I can't go," he says. "Not until I talk to you, Ivy."

"I don't want to hear what you have to say."

"Too damn bad. If you don't let me inside, then I'll just tell you everything through this stupid glass door."

Stubborn ass. "Where's Matt? I thought the appointment was with him."

"He made the appointment so I could come see you." He pauses and takes a deep breath. There are dark circles beneath his eyes, his cheeks are covered in stubble despite him being impeccably dressed in a gorgeous suit, and his hair is mussed. As if he's run his hands through it repeatedly. "Though he really does need your help, Ivy. That winery of his is a disaster."

I love that he's such an admirer of my talents, but it still doesn't change the fact of what he did to me. And how much it hurt. Maybe I overreacted, but so what? I need to be protective of my heart when it comes to Archer. "So you're lying again. Using Matt to see me."

"You won't take my calls, you won't answer my texts. What do you expect me to do?"

"Leave me alone?" I suggest.

He's still shaking his head. "I can't do that."

"Why not?"

"Because I'm in love with you."

My heart cracks wide open. "I don't believe you."

"It's the fucking truth." He grabs the handle of the front door and yanks on it, making the glass rattle. "Open the damn door, Ivy, so I can tell you this sort of thing face to face."

"We are face to face."

"I feel like I'm in goddamn prison, talking to you through the glass." He glares at me, his mouth thin, and I almost want to laugh.

Almost.

I should not open that door. Everyone I know would urge me to tell him to screw off. I don't need his trouble. And he's full of trouble.

But he's also fun . . . and sweet and lovable and sexy and smart. He claims he's in love with me.

I'm in love with him, too.

So I jumped to the worst conclusion, but would anyone blame me? Archer doesn't have the best track record when it comes to women. I wanted to believe he was in love with me, but I was scared. Afraid he'd bail on me after the two weeks we were together because that was our original deal, right? Two weeks. Next thing I know I'm ready to turn it into a lifetime and that's scary.

Maybe I overreacted because I was scared to commit too. Neither of us is perfect.

And then there's that stupid bet Gage told me about. Why didn't Archer mention it from the start? I wouldn't have cared. Those three are always making ridiculous bets with huge payouts. They're ridiculous. The bet is ridiculous.

Yet he kept it from me like some deep dark secret. Doesn't he know I'm used to their behavior by now? And I still love him for it?

He's watching me, his dark eyes looking so haunted I automatically reach out and hit the keypad, punching in the code that deactivates the alarm and flicking the lock so the door can open. Next thing I know he's rushing in, rushing me, and I'm in his arms, being clutched so tight I can hardly breathe as my face is pressed against his chest, breathing in his familiar, delicious scent. He buries his face against my hair, his entire body trembling, and it's like I can't help myself.

I wrap my arms around his solid warmth and close my eyes, savoring being in his arms again.

"I'm sorry," he murmurs against my temple just before he kisses it. "I fucked up and I'm sorry. Will you ever forgive me? I need you to forgive me, Ivy. I need you in my life. I feel lost without you."

Tears threaten. Of course. When do they not threaten lately? "I'm sorry too."

"For what?" He sounds stunned.

"I overreacted. I blamed you and made such a big deal about the bet being a secret but maybe . . . maybe I was scared too." I pull away slightly so we can face each other. It feels so natural, so right, having him here. Touching me, looking at me with all that love and emotion shining in his eyes. It gives me hope. "If you'd been honest about the stupid bet from the beginning, I wouldn't have cared."

He frowns, his brows drawing down. "Really?"

"Archer. I know how you guys operate. I would've helped you win that million dollars if you'd let me in on the secret." I so would've. Not anymore though.

Nope. Now I'm ready to throw him to the wolves and make him pay up.

"I'm an idiot," he says with a sigh. "Your brother said so too."

"You talked to Gage about me?" I'm in shock.

"I wanted his blessing." His face turns solemn, his dark brows drawing together. "Considering I'm in love with his sister, I had to clear the air between us and make sure I had his approval."

"And do you?" I hold my breath for fear of my brother's reaction.

"I do." He smiles faintly, though his jaw is still tight. "I think he gets how much I love you. Thank God. Remember, I'm an idiot when it comes to this sort of thing."

I nod in agreement. He so is. "You are. So am I. Maybe that's why we're so good together."

His expression clears at my words. "I also really messed this up."

"You definitely did."

"You've never, ever been just Ivy to me." He cups my cheek, his fingers drifting lightly across my skin. "You've become my everything."

My heart flutters when he touches the corner of my lips with his thumb. "I've missed you."

"I've missed you too." Leaning in, he kisses me, breathing against my lips all the pent-up hope and love I've held deep inside me as well. "I love you, Ivy. So damn much it's killing me not to have you by my side. I need you. I want you to be my partner in every sense of the word."

"What do you mean?" My heart is beating so fast I swear it's going to thump right out of my chest.

"Come live with me. Work with me. Start your own design business in Napa. Do you know how many calls I've taken since the opening, all of them asking about you? I could give you a ready-made client list."

Pride suffuses me. I had no idea. "Including Matt?"

He chuckles. "Yes. He's reluctant, but I'm trying to sway him. Cheap bastard."

I laugh, feeling lighter than I have in weeks. "What about us?"

Archer sobers immediately. "I'm in love with you, Ivy. I want you by my side forever."

"Forever?" I ask breathlessly

"Yeah." He kisses me again, deeper this time, my lips parting for his persuasive tongue. "Marry me, and we can go into business together. Bancroft and Bancroft," he says after he breaks the kiss.

"Bancroft and Emerson?" I joke, though my head is spinning at his words and what they all mean.

"Baby, if you're going to marry me, you have to take my name. I'm kind of old-fashioned like that." He frowns. "I can't believe I just said that. I sound like a macho ass."

Laughing, I circle my arms around his neck and press my fingers against his nape, forcing him to kiss me again. "I loved that you just said that. I will gladly take your name, Archer. Though I'll be the first Bancroft in Bancroft and Bancroft, I hope you know."

"I don't think so," he murmurs against my smiling lips. "My first name starts with an A. Yours with an I. I'm afraid I'm first."

"Shouldn't you be polite? Ladies first, after all," I tease as he pulls me in closer.

"I think I can do that." He presses his forehead to mine, staring deep into my eyes. "I need to hear you say it, Ivy."

"Say what?" I'm confused. Dazzled. Lost in his dark

brown gaze, those golden flecks dancing with so much happiness.

He doesn't say a word, merely continues to stare at me until realization slowly dawns. "Oh." Tipping my head up, I kiss him. Softly. Reverently. "I forgive you, Archer."

"I forgive you too, Ivy." He's smiling, knowing I'm teasing him, drawing it out. "And?"

"And I love you. So much, I thought I might die without you these last two weeks."

"I feel the same way, baby. The same exact way. Don't ever leave my side again."

"I won't. I promise."

"Become just my wife. Nothing else. Just mine." He's teasing again and this time his words don't hurt.

This time, his declaration fills me with so much love I know he's the man for me.

"Only if you become just my mine too," I say with a smile.

"I already am," he admits. "You own me, Ivy. You own my heart. There's no one else I'd rather belong to."

I kiss him, unable to stand it any longer, my heart and soul completely transformed when I hear him whisper two simple words.

"Just you."

Acknowledgments

As ALWAYS, I'M thanking my husband and children for putting up with me while I work extra hard at my desk, giving myself eyestrain while I stare at the computer all day and night. You are all so awesome and supportive and rarely complain (ha ha). What would I do without you?

To the readers—I would be nothing without your continued enthusiasm and love. Thank you, you all mean the world to me. This book (and this entire series) is a little different, and I hope you love reading it as much as I've enjoyed writing it. Hopefully we can't go wrong with sexy billionaire bachelors . . .

A big thank you to my editor Chelsey Emmelhainz for slapping my words around and making this book so much better. To the entire team at Avon Books for their enthusiastic support of this series—y'all rock. To KP Simmon and Kati Rodriguez for keeping me straight. And to Katy Evans for loving Archer from the very, very beginning.

Can't get enough of the boys with the bet?
Keep reading for a sneak peek at the second
book in Monica Murphy's sexy
Billionaire Bachelors Club series

TORN

Coming in November 2013 from Avon Books

An Excerpt from

TORN

Marina

"TELL ME YOUR name."

A shiver runs down my spine at the commanding, deep voice that sounds in my ear. I keep myself still, trying my best not to react, considering we're surrounded by at least one hundred people, but oh, how I want to.

As in throw myself into the arms of the man who's standing far too close to me, demanding to know my name as if I owe him some sort of favor.

"Tell me yours first," I murmur, turning my head in the opposite direction so it appears I'm not even talking to him. He stands behind me, tall and broad, imposing in his immaculate black suit and crisp white shirt, the silvery tie he wears perfectly knotted at his throat.

I might not be looking at this very moment, but I'd

memorized everything about him from the moment I first saw him not an hour ago. He'd drawn plenty of attention without saying a word, striding into the room as if he owned it, casting that calculating gaze upon all of us in attendance. Looking very much like the mighty king observing his lowly subjects until his eyes lit upon me.

And then he proceeded to watch me for long, agonizing minutes. Butterflies fluttered in my stomach, and for a terrifying moment I wondered if he could see right through me. I shuffled my feet, inwardly cursed myself for coming tonight, but I held firm. I refused to react.

I still refuse to react.

"You don't know who I am?" He sounds amused at the notion, and I'm tempted to walk away without a word. My earlier nerves evaporate. He's so confident, so arrogant, I'm sure he believes he has me.

He doesn't know who he's dealing with then, does he?

Finally I chance a glance at him, drinking in his thick brown hair that's tinged with gold, the way it tumbles across his forehead, his twinkling green eyes, the faint smile that curves his full lips, the combination giving him a boyish appearance. It's a complete illusion because there is nothing boyish about this virile man before me.

"Perhaps you can enlighten me." I offer a carefree smile, the nerves returning tenfold when he takes a step toward me, invading my personal space. His scent hits me first, clean and subtle, a mixture of soap and just . . . him. No cologne that I can detect.

Rather unusual. Most of the men I know slather

themselves in expensive cologne all for the purpose of drawing us silly women in. Instead, they end up choking us out.

With the exception of this man. I find the difference refreshing.

A slow smile appears, revealing perfectly straight white teeth. "Gage Emerson." He thrusts his hand toward me. "And you are?"

He's not very subtle. And he's exactly who I suspected. The very man who recently bought up what feels like half of the Napa Valley, all in the hopes of turning it around and selling it to God knows who just to turn a profit.

Not caring in the least that he's forever changing the landscape of the very place I've grown up in. Devastating my family in the process with his callous buyouts.

"Marina Knight." I sound breathless and I want to smack myself.

A slow, burning anger threads through my veins, and I inhale sharply, desperate to control it. I came here tonight specifically looking for him. And I found him—almost too easily. I knew he was handsome, charming, well spoken. I'd done my research, Googled him for a solid hour trying to find any sort of weakness, but it appeared he had none. Like he's some sort of untouchable superhero.

I didn't expect my reaction toward him, though. My body is humming in all the right places at his closeness. My skin literally tingles, and when he clasps my hand in his to shake it, my knees threaten to buckle.

"A pleasure to meet you, Marina Knight." His voice

rumbles from somewhere deep in his chest and he draws his thumb across the top of my hand in the quickest caress before releasing it.

He's just a man, I remind myself. A dreamy, sexy man, in that polished, overtly masculine, deliciously commanding way that I don't normally find myself drawn to but . . . hmm.

A girl is always allowed to change her mind.

About the Author

Monica Murphy is the wife of one and mother of three. A native Californian, she lives in the foothills below Yosemite but hasn't visited the park in years (whoops). She's also a *USA Today* and *New York Times* bestselling author of new adult and contemporary romances. Visit her online at www.monicamurphyauthor.com and on Facebook at www.facebook.com/MonicaMurphyAuthor.

Visit www.AuthorTracker.com for exclusive information on your favorite HarperCollins authors.

About the Author

A suspense/thriller writer [...] one and another chapter. A [...] to the social networ[...]
in her latest [...] the publisher's [...] pages they offer
a USA Today and [...] Thing is the latest author of
[...] and contemporary romances. S[...] her online
[...] www.[...] or join her on Facebook at
www.facebook.com/[...]

Visit www.AuthorTracker.com for exclusive information
on your favorite HarperCollins authors.

Give in to your impulses . . .
Read on for a sneak peek at four brand-new
e-book original tales of romance
from Avon Books.
Available now wherever e-books are sold.

LESS THAN A GENTLEMAN
By Kerrelyn Sparks

WHEN I FIND YOU
A TRUST NO ONE NOVEL
By Dixie Lee Brown

PLAYING THE FIELD
A DIAMONDS AND DUGOUTS NOVEL
By Jennifer Seasons

HOW TO MARRY A HIGHLANDER
By Katharine Ashe

An Excerpt from

LESS THAN A GENTLEMAN

by Kerrelyn Sparks

New York Times bestselling author
Kerrelyn Sparks returns to romance during
the Revolutionary War with the sequel to her
debut historical novel, *The Forbidden Lady.*

Matthias gazed up the lattice to his balcony. As youngsters, he and his cousin had used the lattice to sneak out at night and go fishing. Of course the doors had not been bolted back then, but climbing down the lattice had seemed more exciting.

Matthias wasn't sure the lattice would hold his weight now, but with Dottie's restorative coursing through him, he felt eager to give it a jolly good try. Halfway up, a thin board cracked beneath his shoe. He shifted his weight and found another foothold. The last thing he wanted was to slip and tear Dottie's stitches from his shoulder.

He swung his legs over the balcony railing and landed with a soft thud. *How odd*. His door was open. *Of course*, he reminded himself. Dottie had gone there to fetch his clothes. She must have opened the door to air out the room.

He slipped inside. Moonlight filtered into the room, glimmering off the white mosquito netting. He strolled over to the secretaire, then kicked off his shoes and dropped his breeches. When he draped the breeches on the back of the chair, he noticed something was already there, something thick. He ran his fingers over the folds of cotton. The scent of roses drifted up to his nose. His mother's perfume. Why would she have left one of her gowns in his room?

Odd. He pulled off his stockings. He'd talk to his mother in the morning. For now, he simply wanted to sink into a mattress and forget about the war.

He unwrapped his neck cloth, then removed his shirt and undergarments. How could he forget the war when he had so much to do? Ferryboats to burn. Supplies to capture. He untied the bow from his hair and dropped the thin leather thong on the desk. And those two missing females. *Where the hell could they be?*

He strode to the bed and slipped under the netting. With a sigh of contentment, he stretched out between the clean cotton sheets.

The bed shifted.

He blinked, staring at the ghostly netting overhead. He hadn't budged an inch. There was only one explanation.

Slowly, he turned his head and peered into the darkness beside him. The counterpane appeared lumpy, as if— He listened carefully. Yes, soft breathing.

He sat up. A soft moan emanated from the form beside him. Female. His heart started to pound, his body reacting instinctively. Good God, it had been too long since he . . .

What the hell? He drew his racing libido to a screeching

halt. This had to be another one of his mother's plots to force him to marry! Even Dottie was in on it. She had insisted he bathe and go to the Great House. Then they had locked up the house, so he would be forced to climb the lattice to his bedchamber. Straight into their trap.

He scrambled out of bed, batting at the mosquito netting that still covered him.

The female gasped and sat up. "Who's there?"

"Bloody hell," he muttered. His mother's scheme had worked perfectly. He was alone and naked with whomever she had chosen for his bride.

Another gasp, and a rustling of sheets. The woman climbed out of bed. Damn! She would run straight to her witnesses to inform them that he'd bedded her.

"No!" He leapt across the bed and grabbed her. "You're not getting away." He hauled her squirming body back onto the bed. Her sudden intake of air warned him of her intent to scream.

He cupped a hand over her mouth. "Don't."

She clamped down with her teeth.

"Ow!" He ripped his hand from her mouth.

She slapped at his shoulders.

He winced as she pounded on his injury. "Enough." He seized her by the wrists and pinned her arms down. "No screaming. And no biting. Do you understand?"

Her breaths sounded quick and frightened.

He settled on top of her, applying just enough pressure to keep her from escaping. "I know what you're after. You think to trap me in wedlock so easily?"

"What?"

He could hardly see her pale face in the dark. His damp hair fell forward, further obstructing his view as he leaned closer. The scent of her soap surrounded him. Magnolia blossoms. His favorite, and Dottie knew it. This was a full-fledged conspiracy. "I assume you brought witnesses with you?"

"Witnesses?"

"Of course. Why would you want me in your bed if there were no one to see it?"

"My God, you're perverse."

"You're hoping I am, aren't you?" He stroked the inside of her wrist. "You're hoping I'll be tempted by your soft skin."

She shook her head and wiggled beneath him.

He gulped. She was definitely not wearing a corset beneath her shift. "You think I cannot resist a beautiful, womanly form?" Damn, but she *was* hard to resist.

"Get off of me," she hissed.

"I beg your pardon? That's hardly the language of a seductress. Didn't they coach you better than that?"

"Damn you, release me."

He chuckled. "You're supposed to coo in my ear, not curse me. Come now, let me hear your pretty little speech. Tell me how much you want me. Tell me how you're burning to make love to me."

"I'd rather burn in hell, you demented buffoon."

He paused, wondering for the first time whether he had misinterpreted the situation. "You're . . . not here to seduce me?"

"Of course not. Why would I have any interest in a demented buffoon?"

He gritted his teeth. "Then who are you and why are you in this bed?"

"I was in bed to sleep, which would be obvious if you weren't such a demented—"

"Enough! Who are you?"

She paused.

"Is the question too difficult?"

She huffed. "I . . . I'm Agatha Ludlow."

An Excerpt from

WHEN I FIND YOU
A TRUST NO ONE NOVEL
by Dixie Lee Brown

Dixie Lee Brown continues her
heart-racing *Trust No One* series with
a sexy veteran determined to protect
an innocent woman on the run.

"Okay—now that I've got your attention, let me tell you about my day." Walker resumed his pacing. "I've been up since four-thirty this morning. I've saved your neck three times so far today, and for my trouble I've been cracked on the skull, threatened by a bear, and nearly drowned. We're through doing it your way." He stopped and pinned her with a warning glance. "I realize you're confused and you've got no idea who I am, but there's only one thing you need to know. I'm taking you out of here with me, and I don't care if I have to throw you over my shoulder and carry you out. Are we clear?"

She watched him without saying a word, looking anything but resigned to her fate.

Walker stared back, daring her to defy him.

She never even flinched.

"If you were me, what would you do?" Her strong, clear voice challenged him, while her eyes flashed with fire.

"If I were you, I'd find someone I could trust and stick with him until this is over."

"And that's you, I suppose? How do I know I can trust you?"

He made a show of looking around. "You don't have a lot of options at the moment, but, in case you haven't noticed, I'm the one trying to keep you alive." He reached for her elbow and pulled her to her feet. The cool breeze through his wet clothes chilled him, and he worried about her. Even with her arms wrapped around herself, just beneath her breasts, she still shook. No sense putting this off. She wasn't magically going to start trusting him in the next few minutes, and they had to get moving.

He held up his jacket in front of her and took a deep breath. "Get out of those wet clothes and put this coat on."

Her eyes widened in alarm and she stared at him, resting her hands on her hips in a stance that would have made him smile if she hadn't been so serious. He held her gaze, expecting her to tell him to go to hell. He couldn't afford to give on this issue, so he kept talking. "We'll head back to higher ground, start a fire, and get our clothes dried out. I have to warm you up, and this is the only way I know to do it. We don't have time to argue about this."

"You can't seriously expect me to . . . you're wet and cold, too. Wear your own damn coat." She wrapped her arms around her waist again, as though she could stop her trembling.

The fear in her expression tugged at his conscience and sent him searching for the words to reassure her that he wasn't going to jump her as soon as she undressed. The suspicious glare she fixed him with succeeded in hardening his resolve, and he lowered the coat, raised an eyebrow, and swept his gaze over her. "Either you can get out of those clothes yourself, or I can help you."

"You wouldn't dare!"

"You'll find there's not too much I wouldn't do."

Darcy glowered at him a few more seconds, clearly wishing she had a tree branch in her hand. Then she sighed and dropped her gaze, blinking several times in quick succession, obviously determined that he wouldn't see her break down. So, the woman wasn't as tough as she wanted him to believe. Her vulnerability unleashed a wave of protectiveness that washed over him and left him feeling like an ass.

He frowned. "I'm not the enemy." He held the coat higher so it blocked his view of everything but her head and shoulders. "Hurry, we have to get moving." Trembling visibly, her lips still maintained a bluish tint. She wasn't out of danger yet.

An Excerpt from

PLAYING THE FIELD
A DIAMONDS AND DUGOUTS NOVEL

by Jennifer Seasons

The sexy baseball players of Jennifer Seasons'
Diamonds and Dugouts series are back
with the story of a single mom, a hot
rookie, and a second chance at love.

An Excerpt from

PLAYING THE FIELD

The sexy baseball players of *Spring Training*,
Diamonds, and *Fastonis* series are back,
with the sexy new novels in the series.

JP reached out an arm to snag her, but she slipped just out of reach—for the moment. Did she really think she could get away from him?

There was a reason he played shortstop in the major leagues. He was damn fast. And now that he'd decided to make Sonny his woman, she was about to find out just how quick he could be. All night he'd tossed and turned for her, his curiosity rampant. When he'd finally rolled out of bed, he'd had one clear goal: to see Sonny. Nothing had existed outside that.

Her leaving her cell phone at the restaurant last night had been the perfect excuse. All he'd had to do was run an internet search for her business to get her address. And now here he was, unexpectedly up close and personal with her. So close he could smell the scent of her shampoo, and it was doing funny things to him. Things like making him want to bury his nose in her hair and inhale.

No way was he going to miss this golden opportunity.

With a devil's grin, he moved and had her back against the aging barn wall before she'd finished gasping. "Look me in the eyes right now and tell me I don't affect you, that you're not interested." He traced a lazy path down the side of her neck with his fingertips and felt her shiver. "Because I don't believe that line for an instant, sunshine."

Close enough to feel the heat she was throwing from her deliciously curved body, JP laughed softly when she tried to sidestep and squeeze free. Her shyness was so damn cute. He raised an arm and blocked her in, his palm flush against the rough, splintering wood. Leaning in close, he grinned when she blushed and her gaze flickered to his lips. Her mouth opened on a soft rush of breath, and, for a suspended moment, something sparked and held between them.

But then Sonny shook back her rose-gold curls and tipped her chin with defiance. "Believe what you want, JP. I don't have to prove anything to you." Her denim blue eyes flashed with emotion. "This might come as a surprise, but I'm not interested in playing with a celebrity like you. I have a business to run and a son to raise. I don't need the headache."

There was an underlying nervousness to her tone that didn't quite jive with the tough-as-nails attitude she was trying to project. Either she was scared or he affected her more than she wanted to admit. She didn't look scared.

JP dropped his gaze to her mouth, wanting to kiss those juicy lips, and felt her body brush against his. He could feel her pulse, fast and frantic, under his fingertips.

It made his pulse kick up a notch in anticipation. "There's a surefire way to end this little disagreement right now, because I say you're lying. I say you *are* interested in a celebrity like me." He cupped her chin with his hand and watched her thick lashes flutter as she broke eye contact. But she didn't pull away. "In fact, I say you're interested in *me*."

JP knew he had her.

Her voice came, soft and a little shaky. "How do I prove I'm not?" The way she was staring at his mouth contradicted her words. So did the way her body was leaning into his.

Lowering his head until he was a whisper away, he issued the challenge, "Kiss me."

Her gaze flew to his, her eyes wide with shock. "You want me to do *what?*"

What he knew they both wanted.

"Kiss me. Prove to me you're not interested, and I'll leave here. You can go back to your business and your son and never see my celebrity ass again."

An Excerpt from

HOW TO MARRY A HIGHLANDER

by Katharine Ashe

In this delightful novella from
award-winning author Katharine Ashe, a
young matchmaker may win the laird of her
dreams if she can manage to find husbands for
seven Scottish ladies—in just one month!

It would have been remarkable if Teresa had not been quivering in her prettiest slippers. Six pairs of eyes stared at her as though she wore horns atop her hat. She was astounded that she had not yet turned and run. Desperation and determination were all well and good when one was sitting in Mrs. Biddycock's parlor, traveling in one's best friend's commodious carriage, and living in one's best friend's comfortable town house. But standing in a strange flat in an alien part of town, anticipating meeting the man one had been dreaming about for eighteen months while being studied intensely by his female relatives, did give one pause.

Her cheeks felt like flame, which was dispiriting; when she blushed, her hair looked glaringly orange in contrast. And this was not the romantic setting in which she had long imagined they would again encounter each other—another ballroom glittering with candlelight, or a rose-trellised garden path in the moonlight, or even a field of waving heather aglow with sunshine. Instead she now stood in a dingy little flat three stories above what looked suspiciously like a gin house.

But desperate times called for desperate measures. She gripped the rim of her bonnet before her and tried to still her nerves.

The sister who had gone to fetch him reappeared in the doorway and smiled. "Here he is, then, miss."

A heavy tread sounded on the squeaking floorboards. Teresa's breath fled.

Then he was standing not two yards away, filling the doorway, and . . .

she . . .

was . . .

speechless.

Even if words had occurred to her, she could not have uttered a sound. Both her tongue and wits had gone on holiday to the colonies.

No wonder she had dreamed.

From his square jaw to the massive breadth of his shoulders to his dark hair tied in a queue, he was everything she had ever imagined a man should be. Aside from the neat whiskers skirting his mouth that looked positively barbaric and thrillingly virile, he was exactly as she remembered him. Indeed, seeing him now, she realized she had not forgotten a single detail of him from that night in the ballroom. She recognized him with the very fibers of her body, as though she already knew how it felt for him to take her hand. Just as on that night eighteen months before, an invisible wind pressed at her back, urging her to move toward him like a magnet drawn to a metal object. *As though they were meant to be touching.*

Despite the momentous tumult within her now, however, Teresa was able to see quite clearly in his intensely blue eyes a stark lack of any recognition whatsoever.

"Weel?" The single word was a booming accusation. "Who be ye, lass, and what do ye be wanting from me?"

It occurred to Teresa that either she could be thoroughly devastated by this unanticipated scenario and subsequently flee in utter shame, or she could continue as planned.

She gripped her bonnet tighter.

"How do you do, my lord? I am Teresa Finch-Freeworth of Brennon Manor at Harrows Court Crossing in Cheshire." She curtseyed upon wobbly legs.

His brow creased. "And?"

"And . . ." It was proving difficult to breathe. "I have come here to offer you my hand in marriage."